Alfred P. Burbank

A Collection of Humorous, Dramatic and Dialect Selections

Alfred P. Burbank

A Collection of Humorous, Dramatic and Dialect Selections

ISBN/EAN: 9783337375386

Printed in Europe, USA, Canada, Australia, Japan

Cover: Foto ©Andreas Hilbeck / pixelio.de

More available books at **www.hansebooks.com**

HUMOROUS, DRAMATIC,

AND

DIALECT SELECTIONS,

EDITED AND ARRANGED

FOR PUBLIC READING OR RECITATION,

BY ALFRED P. BURBANK,

AND CONTAINING MANY CHOICE SELECTIONS NEVER BEFORE IN PRINT, AS
WELL AS SOME OLD FAVORITES.

NEW YORK:

DICK & FITZGERALD, PUBLISHERS.

PREFACE.

I take pleasure in presenting this little volume to the public, as it enables me effectually to answer very many inquiries after choice selections made popular by me and others of the profession, and hitherto most difficult to obtain.

I am especially indebted to Mr. *Dion Boucicault,* for his great kindness in allowing me so liberal an extract from the *Shaugraun;* also to many other kind friends who have, from time to time, suggested or given me some of the rarest bits of dialect in the book.

In preparing this collection, I have taken especial pains to include only those things which *I know by actual trial* to be *strong* and *successful.* Every public reader will appreciate the force of so emphatic a statement as the above, one which I believe can be truthfully made of no other " collection " now extant; and with the experience of nearly one thousand public entertainments in all parts of the country to guide me, I have done my best to fulfill the conditions of preparing an intensely practical and desirable collection.

It will be apparent to all discriminating minds, that this book is by no means intended as a " Reading Book " in the ordinary sense of that term. It is not intended, nor is it fitted, for a school or class text-book; and were it my intention to make this preface, in any sense, an essay on Elocution, I could adduce many reasons why such a book should *not* be so used. It *is* intended to afford both professional and amateur readers a fund of selections especially adapted to the purpose of *entertaining* an audience.

I only regret that the limit of price, and consequent space, in this small book, prevents the introduction of scarcely more than half of my own repertoire, to say nothing of many charming and desirable specialties of other readers, which I might use had I room. Trusting, however, that this book will answer all desirable ends, until it shall seem best to make a more comprehensive collection,

I remain,

The Public's faithful servant,

A. P. BURBANK.

September, 1878.

CONTENTS.

6   CONTENTS.

Recitations and Readings.

CONN'S DESCRIPTION OF THE FOX HUNT.

(From " The Shaugraun "—*Act I, Scene 3.*)

The following extract from the great play of the " Shaugraun " is used with the special permission of Mr. Dion Boucicault. It is taken from the scene where Mrs. O'Kelley, the mother of Conn the Shaugraun (*Irish for vagabond*), is conversing with Conn's sweetheart, pretty little Moya Doolan. As these two women are talking, *enter* Conn.

Mrs. O'Kelley. The polis was in my cabin to-day. They say you stole Squire Foley's horse.

Conn. Well, now, here's a purty thing, for a horse to run away wid a man's character like this. Oh, wurra! may I niver die in sin, but here was the way of it. I was standin' by ould Foley's gate, whin I heard the cry of the hounds comin' across the tail end of the bog, and there they wor, my dear, spread out like the tail of a paycock, and the finest dog fox you ever seen was sailin' ahead of em, up the boreen, an' right across the church-yard. It was enough to rise the inhabitants. Well, as I looked, who should come up an' put her head over the gate beside me, but the squire's brown mare, small blame to her. Divil a thing said I to her, nor she to me, for the hounds had lost their scent among the grave-stones, we knew by their whine and yelp—when, whoop! the fox wint by us. I leapt on the gate, an' gave a shriek of a view-halloo to the *whip*. In a minute the pack caught the scent again, and the

whole field came roarin' past. The mare lost her head and tore
at the gate. Stop, says I, ye divil! and I slipped a taste of a
rope that I had in my pocket over her head an' into her mouth.
Now, mind the cunnin' of the baste. She was quiet in a minute.
Come home aisy, now, says I, an' I threw my leg across her.
Bejabers, no sooner was I on her bare back, than, whoo! holy
rocket! she was over the gate an' tearin' like mad after the hounds.
Yorick, says I, come back, you thief of the world! Tally-ho!
says I, where are you takin' me to? as she went through the
hunting field, and laid me beside the master of the hounds,
Squire Foley himself. He turned the color of his leather breeches.
Mother o' Moses! ses he, is that Conn, the Shaugraun, on my
brown mare? Bad luck to me, ses I, it's no one else. You stole
my horse, ses the Squire. It's a lie, ses I—'twas your horse
stole me.

MOYA. An' what did he say to that?

CONN. I couldn't stop to hear, for just then we took a stone wall
an' a double ditch at the same time, an' he stopped behind to keep
an engagement he had in the ditch.

MRS. O'KELLEY. Ye'll get a month in jail for that.

CONN. A month in jail, will I? Well, begorra, it was worth it.

THE TAILOR'S THIMBLE.

(FROM "THE SHAUGRAUN"—*Act II, Scene* 4.)

On account of Conn's fondness for the "juice of sod" and general dissolute habits, Father Doolan, the parish priest, and uncle of
Conn's sweetheart, Moya, who is her uncle's housekeeper, has quite
forbidden Conn the house; but the young people got together occasionally for all that, and Conn was hanging around outside one
stormy night, as was his custom, when Father Doolan's heart re-
lents and he says:

FATHER DOOLAN. Well, you may let him stand in out of the
wet. Give me a cup of tay, Moya. I hope it will be stronger than
the last. Well, Conn, haven't ye a word to say for yourself?

CONN. Divil a one, yer Riverence.

FATHER DOOLAN. You are goin' to ruin.

CONN. I am, bad luck to me.

FATHER DOOLAN. And you want to take a dacint girl wid ye?

CONN. I'm a vagabone intirely.

FATHER DOOLAN. What sort of a life do ye lead? What is your occupation? Stealin' the salmon out the river at night?

CONN. No, sir, I'm not so bad as that, but I'll confess to a couple of trout—sure the salmon is out o' sayson.

FATHER DOOLAN. The tay smells of whiskey.

CONN. If ye plaze, sir, it's not the tay ye smell, sir—it's me.

FATHER DOOLAN. That reminds me. Didn't ye give me a promise last Easter, a blessed promise made on yer two knees, that ye'd lave off drink?

CONN. I did, barrin' only one thimbleful a day, just to take the cruelty out of the water.

FATHER DOOLAN. One thimbleful? That I allowed you that concession—no more.

CONN. God bless, ye did, an' I kep' my word.

FATHER DOOLAN. Kept your word! how dare ye say that? Didn't I find ye ten days after stretched out as drunk as a fiddler at Tim O'Malley's wake?

CONN. Ye did, bad luck to me.

FATHER DOOLAN. An' ye took only one thimbleful?

CONN. Divil a drop more. Now see this. Ah, will ye listen to me, sir? I'll tell ye how it was. When they axed me to the wake, I wint. Oh, I wouldn't decaive ye, sir—I wint. There was the Mulcaheys an' the Maloneys an' the O'Flahertys an' the Madigans—

FATHER DOOLAN. I don't want to hear about that at all—come to the drink.

CONN. Av coorse. Begorra, I came to that soon enough. Well, sir, whin, after blessin' the keeners an' the rest of them, I couldn't despise a drink out of respect to the corpse, long life to it. But, boys, sez I, I'm on a pinance, sez I. Is there ever a thimble in the house, sez I—for divil a drop more than the full of it will pass my lips this blessed day. Well, as the divil's luck would have it, there was only one thimble in the house and that was a tailor's thimble, an' they couldn't get it full—begorra, they got me full first.

FATHER DOOLAN. Ah, Conn, I'm afeared liquor is not the

worst of your doin's. We've lost sight of you lately for more than six months. In what jail have you spent your time?

CONN. I was on my travels.

FATHER DOOLAN. Where?

CONN. Round the world. Ye see, sir, after Master Robert was tuk an' they sint him away, the heart seemed to go out of me intirely. I'd stand by the say an' look over it, and see the ships sailin' away to were he may be, till the longing grew too big for my body, an' one night I jumped into the coast guard-boat, stuck up the sail, and away I wint.

FATHER DOOLAN. Bless the boy! ye didn't think ye could get to Australia in a skiff?

CONN. I didn't think at all. I wint all night. I tossed about all next day an' that night, till at day-light I come across a big ship. Stop, sez I, an' put me ashore, for the love of Heaven, sez I; I'm out of me coorse. They whipped me on deck. Where d'ye come from? sez the captain. Suilabeg, sez I; I'll be obliged to you if you'll lave me anywhere handy by there. You'll have to go to Melbourne first, sez he. Is that anywhere in the County Sligo, sez I, lookin' like a lamb. If ye heard the shout of laffin' I got for that. Why, ye omadahaun, sez he, ye'll never see yer home for six months. Then I set up a "withersthrue." Poor divil, sez the captain, I'm sorry for you, but ye must cross the say. What work can ye do best? I can play the fiddle, sez I. Take him forward and take good care of him, an' so they did. That's how I got my passage to Australia.

THE O'KELLEY CABIN.

(FROM " THE SHAUGRAUN "—*Act III, Scene* 1.)

Conn's master, the young Irish nobleman, Robert Ffolliot, has been exiled to Australia for his Fenianism. Managing to escape by Conn's assistance, he returns to Ireland, but is quickly apprehended and placed in prison. Conn is equal to the situation and helps him break jail. Just as they are getting nicely away, however, the villain of the play, Corry Kinchella, the cruel squireen, sets upon them with the soldiery and constabulary. Conn outwits them by taking on his master's disguise, so that while the noble-man really escapes, Conn is followed to the ruins of St. Bridget's Abbey, where two shots are fired at him, and he rolls down to the foot of the ruins, apparently dead. It seems that Conn and Ffol-liot had made an appointment with their respective sweethearts, Moya Doolan and Miss Arte O'Neal, to meet them at this spot, and run away with them, provided they get off safely. These two young women are, however, abducted by the villains, and Conn is taken home and laid out on a door, ready for a rale ould Irish wake. Father Doolan is pacing up and down outside the cottage, waiting the arrival of the mourners, and bewailing the untimely fate of poor Conn, and the abduction of Moya and Miss O'Neal, concerning whom he says:

FATHER DOOLAN. These two girls were the only witnesses of the deed. And that was why they were carried off. No one else was present to prove how Conn was killed.

CONN. (*putting head out of window.*) Yis—I was there.

ALL. Conn alive!

CONN. Whist! No, I'm dead.

FATHER DOOLAN. Why, you provoking vagabond, is this the way you play upon our feelings? Are you hurt?

CONN. I've a crack over the lug, an' a scratch across the small of me back. Sure, miss, unless I drawed them two shots, you would never have had the signal.

FATHER DOOLAN. Brave fellow! How did you escape?

CONN. I'll tell you, sir; but, whoo! gorra! they say dead men tell no tales, but here am I, takin' away the character of the cor-poration. When the master got out of the jail, there was Kin-chella and his gang outside, waitin' to murther us. We give them the slip, an' while the master got off, I led them away after me to St. Bridget's Abbey. There, after I got them two shots out of them, I rowled down an' lay as quiet as a sack of pittaties. Miss O'Neal an' Moya were standin' by an' screechin' blue murther. "Stop their mouths!" said a voice that I knew was Kinchella's. Reilly and Sullivan whipped them on to a car that was waitin' out-side. After that, sorra a thing I remimber, till I found myself laid out on a door, wid candles all around me, an' whiskey bottles an' cakes an' sugar an' tobacca an' lemons an' bacon an' snuff, an' the divil an' all. I thought I was in heaven.

FATHER DOOLAN. And that is his idea of heaven! And you let your poor old mother believe you dead, you didn't relieve her sorrow?

CONN. Would ye have me spoil a wake after invitin' all the neighbors? Thin I remimber the polis would be wantin' me for the share I had in helpin' the masther to break jail. Oh, sir, don't let on to the mother; she'd never howld her whist. Besides, sir, I want to be dead, if ye plaze, to folly up the blackguards that have howld of Moya an' Miss O'Neal.

MOL. Do you know the place where these ruffians resort?

CONN. I'm consaited I do.

FATHER DOOLAN. I'll answer for him he knows every disreputable den in the county.

CONN. An' where would ye be now if I didn't?

FATHER DOOLAN. Here comes your mother with the mourners.

CONN. Whoo! she'll find some of the whiskey gone.

THE "OOLAGHAUN."

(FROM "THE SHAUGRAUN"—*Act III, Scene 2.*)

MALE VOICES.

> Och, Oolaghaun! Och, Oolaghaun!
> Make his bed both wide and deep.
> Och, Oolaghaun! Och, Oolaghaun!
> He is only gone to sleep.

FEMALE VOICES.

> Why did ye die—oh, why did ye die,
> And leave us alone to cry?

MALE AND FEMALE VOICES.

> Why did ye die, why did ye die,
> Leaving us to sigh—och, hone!
> Why did ye die, why did ye die,
> Oolaghaun—och, Oolaghaun!

BIDDY MADIGAN. Oh, hoo! Oh, hoo! Oolaghaun! The widdy had a son, an only son—wail for the widdy.

ALL. Oolaghaun!

BIDDY. I seen her when she was a fair young girl, a fair girl wid a child at her breast.

ALL. Oolaghaun!

BIDDY. None was like him, none could compare. (*Aside.*) Give me a drop of something to put the spirit in me—the fire is getting low.

CONN. (*aside.*) It's a mighty pleasant thing to die like this once in awhile, and hear all the good things said about you after yer dead and gone.

BIDDY. He was the pride of the O'Kelleys forevermore.

CONN. I was a big blackguard whin I was alive.

BIDDY. Good and beautiful.

CONN. Oh, go out o' that!

Enter MOLINEAUX.

MOL. I beg pardon for intruding upon this melancholy entertainment—this festive solemnity.

MRS. O'K. Heaven bless yer honor for comin' to see the last of him. Isn't he beautiful?

MOL. The rogue is winking at me.

MRS. O'K. How often I put him to bed as a child, and sung him to sleep; but now he'll be put to bed wid a shovel, and the song was never sung that will awaken him.

MOL. If *any* words could put life into him, I have come to speak them. Robert Ffolliot has been pardoned and returned home a free man.

ALL. Hurra! Hurra!

MOL. But his home is desolate, for the girl he loved has been stolen away. The man who robbed him of his liberty first and then of his estate, has now stolen his betrothed—Mr. Corry Kinchella. The ruffians who shot the brave fellow who lies there were led by Kinchella's agent, Harvey Duff.

ALL. Harvey Duff.

BIDDY. Harvey Duff sent my boy across the sea.

DOYLE. I've a long reckoning agin him and I keep it warm.

MRS. O'K. I've a short one and there he lies.

ALL. Where is he?

MOL. Kinchella and his men are hiding in some den where they hold Miss O'Neale and Moya prisoners.

ALL. Moya Doolan ?

MOL. The niece of your minister, the sweetheart of poor Conn. My men shall aid you in your search; but you are familiar with every nook and corner in the whole county. You must direct it. Robert Ffolliot awaits you at Suilabeg to lead the hunt. That is, after you have paid your melancholy respects to the Shaugraun.

MRS. O'K. No; ye couldn't plaze him better than to go now. Bring back the news that you have revenged his murder, and he'll go under the sod wid a light heart.

(*All exit, except* REILLY, SULLIVAN and CONN.

REILLY. Away wid ye, while I go warn Harvey Duff.

BOTH. Murther alive!

CONN. That's it. Murther alive! That is what I am—a murther that will live to see you both hung for it. I'll be at your wake, and, begorra, I'll give ye both a fine character. (*They rush to the door.*) Aisy, boys, aisy; the door is fast, and here's the key; ye're in a fine trap. Oho! ye made a mistake last night.

REILLY. Did ye forget that ye are dead ?

SULLIVAN. Sure, if we made a mistake last night, we can repair it now.

CONN. Oh, tare an' ages, what'll I do ?

REILLY. We'll just lay ye out comfortable again, where ye wor; divil a sowl will be any the wiser.

CONN. *Help! help!*

REILLY. They are all miles away by this time; screechin' won't save ye.

CONN. Help! help!

SULL. Shut the windy. I'll quiet him.

MOL. (*at window.*) Drop those knives! Do you hear what I said ? Drop those knives! Now open the door.

CONN. Yes, here's the kay.

MOL. If you put your head outside that cabin, I'll put a bullet in it.

CONN. (*to* SULLIVAN.) Help me up; the hangman will do as much for you some day.

MOL. What men are these ?

CONN. A couple of Kinchella's chickens; they know the road we want to travel.

MOL. Take that pistol—do you know how to use it ?

CONN. I'll try.

MOL. Attention! attention! Put your hands in your pockets.

    *   *   *   *   *   *

Now take me right to where your employer, Mr. Kinchella, has imprisoned Miss O'Neal and Moya, and if on the road you take your hands out of your pockets, or attempt to move beyond the reach of my sword, upon my honor, as an officer and a gentleman, I'll cut you down. *Forward!*

CONN. Attention! Put your hand in my pocket. Now take me straight to where Moya Doolan's shut up, and if you stir a peg out o' that on the road, by the piper that played before Julius Cæsar, I'll save the county six feet of rope.

RIP VAN WINKLE.

PART I.

The following scene is taken from the first act of the celebrated play of RIP VAN WINKLE, as recited by Mr. Burbank, with the special permission of Mr. Joseph Jefferson.

The language is but slightly altered and adapted from the original, to make it more manageable as a monologue.

The characters introduced are—

RIP VAN WINKLE.

DERRICK VON BEEKMAN, *the villain of the play, who endeavors to get* RIP *drunk, in order to have him sign away his property to* VON BEEKMAN.

NICK VEDDER, *the village inn-keeper.*

SCENE.—*The Village Inn.*

Present, VON BEEKMAN, *alone.*

Enter RIP, *shaking off the* CHILDREN, *who cling about him like flies to a lump of sugar*

RIP. (*to the* CHILDREN.) Say! hullo, dere, du Yacob Stein! du kleine spitzboob. Let dat dog Schneider alone, will you? Dere, I tole you dat all de time, if you don'd let him alone he's goin' to

bide you! Why, hullo, Derrick! how you was? Ach, my!
Did you hear dem liddle fellers just now? Dey most plague mo
crazy. Ha, ha, ha! I like to laugh my outsides in every timo I
tink about it. Just now, as we was comin' along togedder, Schneider and me—I don'd know if you know Schneider myself? Well,
he's my dog. Well, dem liddle fellers, dey took Schneider, und—
ha, ha, ha!—dey—ha, ha!—dey *tied a tin kettle mit his tail!* Ha,
ha, ha! My gracious! of you had seen dat dog run! My, how
scared he was! Vell, he was a-runnin' an' de kettle was a-bangin'
an'—ha, ha, ha! you believe it, dat dog, he run right *betwixt mo
an' my legs!* Ha, ha, ha! Ile spill me und all dem liddle fellers
down in de mud togedder. Ha, ha, ha!

VON BEEKMAN. Ah, yes, that's all right, Rip, very funny, very
funny; but what do you say to a glass of liquor, Rip?

RIP. Well, now, Derrick, what do I generally say to a glass?
I generally say it's a good ting, don'd I? Und I generally say a
good deal more to what is *in* it, dan to de glass.

VON B. Certainly, certainly! Say, hallo, there! Nick Vedder,
bring out a bottle of your best!

RIP. Dat's right—fill 'em up. You wouldn't believe it, Derrick,
but dat is de first one I have had to-day. I guess maybe de
reason is, I couldn't got it before. Ah, Derrick, my score is too
big! Well, here is your good health und your family's—may
they all live long und prosper. (*They drink.*) Ach! you may well
smack your lips, und go ah, ah! over *dat* liquor. You don'd give
me such liquor like dat every day, Nick Vedder. Well, come on,
fill 'em up again. Git out mit dat water, Nick Vedder, I don'd
want no water in my liquor. Good liquor und water, Derrick, is
just like man und wife, *dey don'd agree well togedder*—dat's me
und *my* wife, any way. Well, come on again. Here is your good
health und your family's, und may dey all live long und prosper!

NICK VEDDER. That's right, Rip; drink away, and "drown your
sorrows in the flowing bowl."

RIP. Drown my sorrows? Ya, dat's all very well, but *she don'd
drown.* My wife is my sorrow und you can't drown her; she tried
it once, but she couldn't do it. What, didn't you hear about dat,
de day what Gretchen she like to got drownded? Ach, my; dat's
de funniest ting in de world. I'll tell you all about it. It was de
same day what we got married. I bet you I don'd forgot *dat* day so

long what I live. You know dat Hudson River what dey git dem boats over—well, dat's de same place. Well, you know dat boat what Gretchen she was a-goin' to come over in, dat got *upsetted*— ya, just went righd by der boddom. *But she wasn't in de boat.* Oh, no; if she had been in de boat, well, den, maybe she might have got drownded. You can't tell anyting at all about a ting like dat!

VON B. Ah, no; but I'm sure, Rip, if Gretchen were to fall into the water now, you would risk your life to save her.

RIP. *Would I?* Well, I am not so sure about dat myself. When we was first got married ? Oh, ya; I know I would have done it den, but I don'd know how it would be now. But it would be a good deal more my duty now as it was den. Don'd you know, Derrick, when a man gits married a long time—mit his wife, he gits a good deal attached mit her, und it would be a good deal more my duty now as it was den. But I don'd know, Derrick. I am afraid if Gretchen should fall in de water now und should say, "Rip, Rip! help me oud"—I should say, "Mrs. Van Winkle, I will just go home und tink about it." Oh, no, Derrick; if Gretchen fall in de water now she's got to swim, I told you dat— ha, ha, ha, ha! Hullo! dat's her a-comin' now; I guess it's bedder I go oud! (*Exit* RIP.

PART II.

Shortly after his conversation with Von Beekman, Rip's wife catches him carousing and dancing upon the village green with the pretty girls. She drives him away in no very gentle fashion, and he runs away from her only to go and get drunker than before. Returning home after nightfall in a decidedly muddled condition, he puts his head through the open window at the rear, not observing his irate wife, who stands in ambush behind the clothes-bars with her ever-ready broomstick, to give him a warm reception; but seeing only his little daughter Meenie, of whom he is very fond, and who also loves him very tenderly, RIP says:

Meenie! Meenie, my darlin'!

MEENIE. Hush-sh-h.

(*Shaking finger, to indicate the presence of her mother.*

RIP. Eh! what's de matter? I don'd see noting, my darlin'.

MEENIE. 'Sh-sh-sh!

RIP. Eh! what? Say, Meenie, is de ole wild cat home? (GRET-CHEN *catches him quickly by the hair.*) Oh, oh! say, is dat you, Gretchen? Say, dere, my darlin', my angel, don'd do dat. Let go my head, wond you? Well, den, hold on to it so long what you like. (GRETCHEN *releases him.*) Dere, now, look at dat, see what you done—you gone pull out a whole handful of hair. What you want to do a ting like dat for? You must want a bald-headed husband, don'd you?

GRETCHEN. Who was that you called a wild cat?

RIP. Who was dat I call a wild cat? Well, now, let me see, who was dat I call a wild cat? Dat must a' been de same time I come in de winder dere, wasn't it? Yes, I know, it was de same time. Well, now, let me see. (*Suddenly.*) It was de dog Schneider dat I call it.

GRETCHEN. The dog Schneider? That's a likely story.

RIP. Why, of course it is a likely story—ain't he my dog? Well, den, I call him a wild cat just so much what I like, so dere now. (GRETCHEN *begins to weep.*) Oh, well; dere, now, don'd you cry, don'd you cry, Gretchen; you hear what I said? Lisden now. If you don'd cry, I nefer drink anoder drop of liquor in my life.

GRETCHEN. (*crying.*) Oh, Rip! you have said so so many, many times, and you never kept your word yet.

RIP. Well, I say it dis time, and I mean it.

GRETCHEN. Oh, Rip! if I could only trust you.

RIP. You mustn't *suspect* me. Can't you see repentance in my eye?

GRETCHEN. Rip, if you will only keep your word, I shall be the happiest woman in the world.

RIP. You can believe it. I nefer drink anoder drop so long what I live, if you don'd cry.

GRETCHEN. Oh, Rip, how happy we shall be! And you'll get back all the village, Rip, just as you used to have it; and you'll fix up our little house so nicely; and you and I, and our darling little Meenie, here—how happy we shall be!

RIP. Dere, dere, now! you can be just so happy what you like. Go in de odder room, go along mit you; I come in dere pooty quick. (*Exit* GRETCHEN *and* MEENIE.) My! I swore off fon drinkin' so many, many times, and I never kep' my word yet.

(*Taking out bottle.*) I don'd believe dere is more as one good drink in dat bottle, anyway. It's a pity to waste it! You goin' to drink dat? Well, now, if you do, it is de last one, remember dat, old feller. Well, here is your goot held, und—

Enter GRETCHEN, *suddenly, who snatches the bottle from him.*

GRETCHEN. Oh, you brute! you paltry thief!

RIP. Hold on dere, my dear, you will spill de liquor.

GRETCHEN. Yes, I *will* spill it, you drunken scoundrel! (*Throwing away the bottle.*) *That's the last drop you ever drink under this roof.*

RIP. (*slowly, after a moment's silence, as if stunned by her severity.*) Eh! what?

GRETCHEN. Out, I say! you drink no more here.

RIP. What? Gretchen, are you goin to drive me away?

GRETCHEN. Yes! Acre by acre, foot by foot, you have sold everything that ever belonged to you for liquor. Thank Heaven this house is mine, and you can't sell it.

RIP. (*rapidly sobering, as he begins to realize the gravity of the situation.*) Yours? yours? Ya, you are right—it is yours; I have got no home. (*In broken tones, almost sobbing.*) But where will I go?

GRETCHEN. Anywhere! out into the storm, to the mountains. There's the door—never let your face darken it again.

RIP. What, Gretchen! are you goin' to drive me away like a dog on a night like dis?

GRETCHEN. Yes; out with you! *You have no longer a share in me or mine.* (*Breaking down and sobbing with the intensity of her passion.*

RIP. (*very slowly and quietly, but with great intensity.*) Well, den, I will go; you have drive me away like a dog, Gretchen, and I will go. But remember, Gretchen, after what you have told me here to-night, I can never come back. You have open de door for me to go; you will never open it for me to return. But, Gretchen, you tell me dat I have no longer a share here. (*Points at the child, who kneels crying at his feet.*) Good-by, (*with much emotion*) my darlin'. God bless you! Don'd you nefer forgit your fader. Gretchen, (*with a great sob*) I wipe de disgrace from your door. Good-by, good-by! (*Exit* RIP *into the storm.*

THE DEATH OF THE OLD SQUIRE.

Read with great success by CHARLOTTE CUSHMAN.

'Twas a wild, mad kind of night, as black as the bottomless pit;
The wind was howling away like a Bedlamite in a fit,
Tearing the ash boughs off, and mowing the poplars down,
In the meadows beyond the old flour mill, where you turn off to
    the town.

And the rain (well, it *did* rain) dashing against the window glass,
And deluging on the roof, as the Devil were come to pass;
The gutters were running in floods outside the stable door,
And the spouts splashed from the tiles, as they would never give
    o'er.

Lor', how the winders rattled! you'd almost ha' thought that
    thieves
Were wrenching at the shutters, while a ceasles pelt of leaves
Flew to the doors in gusts; and I could hear the beck
Falling so loud I knew at once it was up to a tall man's neck.

We was huddling in the harness-room, by a little scrap of fire,
And Tom, the coachman, he was there, a-practicing for the choir;
But it sounded dismal, anthem did, for Squire was dying fast,
And the doctor said, do what he would, Squire's breaking up at last.

The death-watch, sure enough, ticked loud just over th' owd
    mare's head,
Though he had never once been heard up there since master's boy
    lay dead;
And the only sound, beside Tom's toon, was the stirring in the
    stalls,
And the gnawing and the scratching of the rats in the owd walls.

We couldn't hear Death's foot pass by, but we knew that he was
    near,
And the chill rain and the wind and cold made us all shake with
    fear;
We listened to the clock up-stairs, 'twas breathing soft and low,
For the nurse said, at the turn of night the old Squire's soul would go.

Master had been a wildish man, and led a roughish life ;
Didn't he shoot the Bowton squire, who dared write to his wife ?
He beat the Rads at Hindon Town, I heard, in twenty-nine,
When every pail in market place was brimmed with red port wine.

And as for hunting, bless your soul, why, for forty year or more
He'd kept the Marley hounds, man, as his fayther did afore ;
And now to die, and in his bed—the season just begun—
"It made him fret," the doctor said, "as it might do any one."

And when the young sharp lawyer came to see him sign his will,
Squire made me blow my horn outside as we were going to kill ;
And we turned the hounds out in the court—that seemed to do
        him good ;
For he swore, and sent us off to seek a fox in Thornhill Wood.

But then the fever it rose high and he would go see the room
Where mistress died ten years ago when Lammastide shall come ;
I mind the year, because our mare at Salisbury broke down ;
Moreover, the town-hall was burnt at Steeple Dinton Town.

It might be two, or half-past two, the wind seemed quite asleep ;
Tom, he was off, but I, awake, sat watch and ward to keep ;
The moon was up, quite glorious like, the rain no longer fell,
When all at once out clashed and clanged the rusty turret bell.

That hadn't been heard for twenty year, not since the Luddite days.
Tom he leaped up, and I leaped up, for all the house a-blaze
Had sure not scared us half so much, and out we ran like mad,
I, Tom and Joe, the whipper-in, and t' little stable lad.

" He's killed himself," that's the idea that came into my head ;
I felt as sure as though I saw Squire Barrowly was dead ;
When all at once a door flew back, and he met us face to face ;
His scarlet coat was on his back, and he looked like the old race.

The nurse was clinging to his knees, and crying like a child ;
The maids were sobbing on the stairs, for he looked fierce and
        wild ;
" Saddle me Lightning Bess, my men," that's what he said to me ;
" The moon is up, we're sure to find at Stop or Etterly.

" Get out the dogs ; I'm well to-night, and young again and sound,
I'll have a run once more before they put me under ground ;

They brought my father home feet first, and it never shall be said
That his son Joe, who rode so straight, died quietly in his bed.

"Brandy!" he cried; "a tumbler full, you women howling there;"
Then clapped the old black velvet cap upon his long gray hair,
Thrust on his boots, snatched down his whip, though he was old
    and weak;
There was a devil in his eye that would not let me speak.

We loosed the dogs to humor him, and sounded on the horn;
The moon was up above the woods, just east of Haggard Bourne;
I buckled Lightning's throat-lash fast; the Squire was watching
    me;
He let the stirrups down himself so quick, yet carefully.

Then up he got and spurred the mare, and, ere I well could mount,
He drove the yard gate open, man, and called to old Dick Blount,
Our huntsman, dead five years ago —for the fever rose again,
And was spreading like a flood of flame fast up into his brain.

Then off he flew before the dogs, yelling to call us on,
While we stood there, all pale and dumb, scarce knowing he was
    gone;
We mounted, and below the hill we saw the fox break out,
And down the covert ride we heard the old Squire's parting shout.

And in the moonlit meadow mist we saw him fly the rail
Beyond the hurdles by the beck, just half way down the vale;
I saw him breast fence after fence—nothing could turn him back;
And in the moonlight after him streamed out the brave old pack.

'Twas like a dream, Tom cried to me, as we rode free and fast,
Hoping to turn him at the brook, that could not well be passed,
For it was swollen with the rain; but ah, 'twas not to be;
Nothing could stop old Lightning Bess but the broad breast of the
    sea.

The hounds swept on, and well in front the mare had got her
    stride;
She broke across the fallow land that runs by the down side;
We pulled up on Chalk Linton Hill, and, as we stood us there,
Two fields beyond we saw the Squire fall stone dead from the mare.

Then she swept on, and in full cry the hounds went out of sight ;
A cloud came over the broad moon and something dimmed our
sight,
As Tom and I bore master home, both speaking under breath ;
And that's the way I saw th' owd Squire ride boldly to his death.

SCHNEIDER'S DESCRIPTION OF THE PLAY OF LEAH.

I vant to dold you vat it is, dot's a putty nice play. De
first dime dot you see Leah, she runs cross a pridge, mit
some fellers chasin' her mit putty big shticks. Dey *ketch*
her right in de middle of der edge, und her leader (dot's de
villen) he sez of her, " Dot it's better ven she *dies*, und dot
he coodent allow it dot she can *lif.*" Und de *oder* fellers
hollers out, " So ve vill;" " Give her some deth ;" " Kill
her putty quick ;" " Shmack her of der jaw," und such
dings ; und chust as dey vill kill her, de priest says of dem,
" Don'd you do dot," und dey shtop dot putty quick. In
der nexd seen, dot Leah meets Rudolph (dot's her feller)
in de voods. Before dot he comes in, she sits of de bottom
of a cross, und she don't look putty *lifely*, und she says,
" Rudolph, Rudolph, how is dot, dot you don'd come und
see aboud me ? You didn't shpeak of me for tree days
long. I vant to dold you vot it is, dot ain't some luf. I
don'd like dot." Vell, Rudolph he don'd vas dere, so he
coodent sed something. But ven he comes in, she dells of
him dot she lufs him *orful*, und he says dot he guess he
lufs her orful too, und vants to know vood she leef dot
place, und go oud in some oder country mit him. Und she
says, " I told you, I vill ;" und he says, " Dot's all right,"
und he tells her he vill meet her soon, und dey vill go vay
dogedder. Den he *kisses* her und goes oud, und she feels
honkey dorey 'bout dot.

Vell, in der nexd seen, Rudolph's old man finds oud all aboud dot, und he don'd feel putty *goot;* und he says of Rudolph, "Vood you leef *me,* und go mit dot gal?" und Rudolph feels putty bad. He don'd know vot he shall do. Und der old man he says, "I dold you vot I'll do. Do skoolmaster (dot's de villen) says dot she mighd dook some money to go vay. Now, Rudolph, my poy, I'll give de skoolmaster some money to gif do her, und if she don'd dook dot money, I'll let you marry dot gal." Ven Rudolph hears dis, he chumps mit joyness, und says, "Fader, fader, dot's all righd. I baed you anydings she woodent dook dot money." Vell, de old man gif de skoolmaster de money, und dells him dot he shall offer dot of her. Vell, dot pluddy skoolmaster comes back und says dot Leah dook dot gold righd avay ven she didn't do dot. Den de old man says, "Didn't I told you so?" und Rudolph gets so vild dot he svears dot she can't haf someding more to do mit him. So ven Leah vill meet him in de voods, he don'd vas dere, und she feels orful, und goes avay. Bime-by she comes up to Rudolph's house. She feels putty bad, and she knocks of de door. De old man comes oud, und says, "Got oud of dot, you orful vooman. Don'd you come round after my poy again, else I put you in de dooms." Und she says, "Chust let me see Rudolph vonce, und I vill vander avay." So den Rudolph comes oud, und she vants to rush of his arms, but dot pluddy fool voodent allow dot. He chucks her avay, und says, "Don'd you touch me uf you please, you deceitfulness gal." I dold you vat it is, dot looks *ruff* for dot poor gal. Und she is extonished, und says, "Vot is dis aboud dot?" Und Rudolph, orful mad, says, "Got oudsiedt, you ignomonous vooman." Und she feels so orful she coodent said a vord, und she goes oud.

Afterwards, Rudolph gits married to anoder gal in a shurch. Vell, Leah, who is vandering eferyveres, happens to go in dot shurch-yard to cry, chust at de *same* dime of Rudolph's marriage, which she don'd know someding

aboud. Putty soon she hears de organ, und she says dere
is some beeples gitten married, und dot it vill do her un-
happiness goot if she sees dot. So she looks in de vinder,
und ven she sees who dot is, my graciousness, don'd she
holler, und shvears vengeance! Putty soon Rudolph
chumps oud indo der shurch-yard to got some air. He says
he don'd feel putty goot. Putty soon dey see each oder,
und dey had a orful dime. He says of her, " Leah, how is
dot you been here?" Und she say mit big scornfulness,
" How is dot, you got cheek to talk of me afder dot vitch
you hafe done?" Den he says, " Vell, vot for you dook
dot gold, you false-hearted leetle gal?" Und she says,
" Vot gold is dot? I didn't dook some gold." Und he
says, " Don'd you dold a lie aboud dot?" She says slow-
fully, " I dold you I didn't dook some gold. Vot gold is
dot?" Und den Rudolph tells her all aboud dot, und she
says, " Dot is a orful *lie*. I didn't seen some gold;" und
she adds mit much sarkasmness, " Und you beliefed I dook
dot gold? Dot's de vorst I efer heered. Now, on account
of dot, I vill give you a few gurses." Und den she svears
mit orful voices dot Mister Kain's gurse should git on him,
und dot he coodent never git any happiness eferyvere, no
matter vere he is. Den she valks off. Vell, den a long
dime passes avay, und den you see Rudolph's farm. He
has got a nice vife, und a putiful leetle child. Purty soon
Leah comes in, being shased, as ushual, by fellers mit
shticks. She looks like she didn't ead someding for two
monds. Rudolph's wife sends off dot mop, und Leah gits
avay again. Den dot nice leetle child comes oud, und
Leah comes back ; und ven she sees dot child, don'd she
feel orful aboud dot, und she says mit affectfulness, " Come
here, leedle child, I vooden'd harm you ;" und dot nice
leedle child goes righd up, und Leah grabs her in her arms,
und gries, und kisses her. Oh, my graciousness, don'd she
grie aboud dot!

Und den she say vile she gries, " Leedle childs, don'd

you got some names?" Und dot leedle child shpeaks oud
so nice, piess her leedle hard, und says, "Oh, yes. My
name, dot's Leah, and my papa tells me dot I shall pray
for you efery nighd." Oh, my goodnessness, don'd Leah
gry orful ven she hears dot! I dold you vot it is, dot's a
shplaindid ding. Und quick comes dem tears in your
eyes, und you look up at de vall, so dot nobody can'd see
dot, und you make oud you don'd care aboud it. But your
eyes gits fulled up so quick dot you couldn'd keep dem in,
und de tears comes down of your face like a shnow-storm,
und den you don'd care if eferybody sees dot. Und Leah
kisses her und gries like dot her heart's broke, und she
dooks off dot gurse from Rudolph and goes avay. De child
den dell her fader und muder aboud dot, und dey pring
her pack. Den dot mop comes back und vill kill her again,
but she exposes dot skoolmaster, dot villain, und dot fixes
him. Den she falls down in Rudolph's arms, und your eyes
gits fulled up again, and you can'd see someding more.
You couldn't help dot any vay. Und if I see a gal vot don'd
gry in dot piece, I voodn't marry dot gal, efen if her fader
owned a pig prewery. But I told you vat it is, dot's a
putty piece.   UNCLE SCHNEIDER.

LOVE ON THE HALF-SHELL.

A Ballad of Oyster Bay.   D. L. PROUDFIT.

[This selection should be read with a moderate stutter.]

I ain't anybody in particular,
   And never cal'clated to be ;
I'm aware that my views doesn't signify
   Except to Belinda and me ;
But I'm heavy on openin' oysters—
   In regards to them I am free

To remark that for shellin' of Blue Points,
  There is few that can lay over me.

Excuse my perfessional blowin',
  It isn't the point I would make,
But I'm feelin' particular airy,
  And uncommonly wide awake ;
And I've got to be talkin' about it,
  It won't lay quiet, you see ;
Which the name of the girl is Belinda,
  That's took an affection for me.

It's surprisin'—the fact is surprisin'—
  Just cast your eye over this frame !
Is there anything 'specially gallus
  Which characterizes the same ?
As a model for makin' wax figgers
  I shouldn't make much of a stir ;
But I ain't a-goin' to worry,
  So long as I'm pleasin' to her.

An impediment hinders my speakin'
  As I should admire to do ;
As an elocutin' perfessor
  My scholars would likely be few ;
But she said, when I mentioned it to her,
  " Why, dear, don't you fret, for, you see,
You tell me you love me, my darling,
  And your voice is like music to me."

I was never indicted for intellect,
  Nor never arrested for cheek ;
But I'm holdin' my head elevated
  Since Thursday night was a week ;
For that wus the date when Belinda
  Allowed she was partial to me,
And give me a relish for livin',
  And a notion of workin' for she.

She isn't egzactly a beauty,
  And also she uses a crutch ;

But the eyes of that dear little cripple
 The heart of an oyster would touch.
They is wonderful soft, and so lovin',
 A good-lookin' face on the whole,
Fur the light in them eyes seems to travel
 Right out from a beautiful soul.

If she had been lively and hearty
 I couldn't have helped her, you see;
And similar, then, it ain't likely
 That she would have took up with me;
And I shouldn't have knowed her and loved her,
 So patient and gentle and sweet;
And I wish that the whole of creation
 I could lay at her poor little feet.

I was never so chirk and galloptious,
 And never before felt so spry;
And I've just took to noticin' lately
 How amazin'ly blue is the sky;
And how gay is the stars in the night-time,
 A-winkin' and glimmerin' down—
Good gracious! I come near forgettin'
 That barrel of oysters for Brown!

———

FATHER PHIL'S COLLECTION.

SAMUEL LOVER.

Abridged for Public Reading.

Father Blake was more familiarly known by the name
of Father Phil. By either title, or in whatever capacity, the
worthy Father had great influence over his parish, and
there was a free-and-easy way with him, even in doing the
most solemn duties, which agreed wonderfully with the
devil-may-care spirit of Paddy. Stiff and starched formality in any way is repugnant to the very nature of Irish-
men. There are forms, it is true, and many in the Romish

Church, but they are not *cold* forms, but *attractive* rather, to a sensitive people; besides, I believe those very forms, when observed the least formally, are the most influential on the Irish.

With all his intrinsic worth, Father Phil was, at the same time, a strange man in exterior manners; for with an abundance of real piety, he had an abruptness of delivery, and a strange way of mixing up an occasional remark to his congregation in the midst of the celebration of the mass, which might well startle a stranger; but this very want of formality made him beloved by the people, and they would do ten times as much for Father Phil as for the severe Father Dominick.

On the Sunday in question Father Phil intended delivering an address to his flock from the altar, urging them to the necessity of bestirring themselves in the repairs of the chapel, which was in a very dilapidated condition, and at one end let in the rain through its worn-out thatch. A subscription was necessary; and to raise this among a very impoverished people was no easy matter. The weather happened to be unfavorable, which was most favorable to Father Phil's purpose, for the rain dropped its arguments through the roof upon the kneeling people below, in the most convincing manner; and as they endeavored to get out of the wet, they pressed round the altar as much as they could, for which they were reproved very smartly by his Reverence in the very midst of the mass. These interruptions occurred sometimes in the most serious places, producing a ludicrous effect, of which the worthy Father was quite unconscious, in his great anxiety to make the people repair the chapel.

A big woman was elbowing her way towards the rails of the altar, and Father Phil, casting a sidelong glance at her, sent her to the right-about, while he interrupted his appeal to Heaven to address her thus:

" *Agnus Dei*— You'd betther jump over the rails of the

althar, I think. Go along out o' that, there's plenty o'
room in the chapel below there—"

Then he would turn to the altar, and proceed with the
service, till, turning again to the congregation, he perceived some fresh offender.

" *Orate, fratres !*.— Will you mind what I say to you,
and go along out o' that ? There's room below there. Thrue
for you, Mrs. Finn—it's a shame for him to be thramplin'
on you. Go along, Darby Casy, down there, and kneel in
the rain—it's a pity you haven't a decent woman's cloak
under you, indeed ! *Orate, fratres !*"

* * * * * * *

Again he turned to pray, and after some time he made
an interval in the service to address his congregation on
the subject of the repairs, and produced a paper containing the names of subscribers to that pious work who had
already contributed, by way of example to those who
had not.

" Here it is," said Father Phil—" here it is, and no deny-
ing it—down in black and white ; but if they who give are
down in black, how much blacker are those who have not
given at all ! But I hope they will be ashamed of themselves when I howld up those to honor who have contributed to the uphowlding of the house of God.   And isn't it
ashamed o' yourselves you ought to be, to lave His house
in such a condition ? and doesn't it rain a'most every Sunday, as if He wished to remind you of your duty ? aren't
you wet to the skin a'most every Sunday ? Oh, God is
good to you ! to put you in mind of your duty, giving you
such bitther cowlds that you are coughing and sneezin' every
Sunday to that degree that you can't hear the blessed
mass for a comfort and a benefit to you ; and so you'll go
on sneezin' until you put a good thatch on the place, and
prevent the appearance of the evidence from Heaven
against you every Sunday, which is condemning you before
your faces, and behind your backs too, for don't I see this

minute a strame o' wather that might turn a mill running down Micky Mackavoy's back, between the collar of his coat and his shirt ?"

Here a laugh ensued at the expense of Micky Mackavoy, who certainly *was* under a very heavy drip from the imperfect roof.   .

" And is it laughin' you are, you haythens ?" said Father Phil, reproving the merriment which he himself had pur· posely created, *that he might reprove it.* " Laughin' is it you are, at your backslidings and insensibility to the honor of God—laughin' because when you come here to be saved, you are lost entirely with the wet; and how, I ask you, are my words of comfort to enter your hearts when the rain is pouring down your backs at the same time ?   Sure I have no chance of turning your hearts while you are uudher rain that might turn a mill—but once put a good roof on the house, and I will inundate you with piety ! Maybe it's Father Dominick you would like to have coming among you, who would grind your hearts to powdher with his heavy words." (Here a low murmur of dissent ran through the throng.)   " Ha, ha ! so you wouldn't like it, I see—very well, very well—take care, then, for if I find you insensible to my moderate reproofs, you hard-hearted haythens, you malefacthors and cruel persecuthors, that won't put your hands in your pockets because your mild and quiet poor fool of a pasthor has no tongue in his head ! I say, your mild, quiet poor fool of a pasthor (for I know my own faults partly, God forgive me !) and I can't spake to you as you deserve, you hard-living vagabonds, that are as insensible to your duties as you are to the weather.   I wish it was sugar or salt that you were made of, and then the rain might melt you if *I* couldn't ; but no, them naked rafthers grins in your face to no purpose—you chate the house of God—but take care, maybe you won't chate the divil so aisy." (Here there was a sensation.)   " Ha, ha ! that makes you open your ears, does it ?   More shame for you ;

you ought to despise that dirty enemy of man, and depend
on something better—but I see I must call you to a sense
of your situation with the bottomless pit undher you, and
no roof over you. Oh, dear! dear! dear! I'm ashamed
of you—throth, if I had time and sthraw enough, I'd rather
thatch the place myself than lose my time talking to you;
sure the place is more like a stable than a chapel. Oh,
think of that! the house of God to be like a stable! for
though our Redeemer was born in a stable, that is no reason why you are to keep his house always like one.

"And now I will read you the list of subscribers, and it
will make you ashamed when you hear the names of several
good and worthy Protestants in the parish, and out of it,
too, who have given more than the Catholics."

     *   *   *   *   *   *   *

SUBSCRIPTION LIST

For the Repairs and Enlargement of Ballysloughgutthery Chapel.

Philip Blake, P. P.

Micky Hickey, £0 7s. 6d. "He might as well have
made it ten shillings; but half a loaf is betther than no
bread."

" Plaze your Reverence," says Mick, from the body of
the chapel, " sure seven and sixpence is more than the half
of ten shillings." (A laugh.)

" Oh, how witty you are! Faith, if you knew your
prayers as well as your arithmetic, it would be betther for
you, Micky."

Here the Father turned the laugh against Mick."

Billy Riley, £0 3s. 4d. " Of course he means to sub-
scribe again!"

John Dwyer, £0 15s. 0d. "That's something like! I'll
be bound he's only keeping back the odd five shillings for
a brush full o' paint for the althar; it's as black as a crow,
instead o' being white as a dove."

He then hurried over rapidly some small subscribers as follows:

Peter Hefferman, £0 1s. 8d.

James Murphy, £0 2s. 6d.

Mat Donovan, £0 1s. 3d.

Luke Dannely, £0 3s. 0d.

Jack Quigly, £0 2s. 1d.

Pat Finnegan, £0 2s. 2d.

EDWARD O'CONNOR, Esq., £2 0s. 0d. " There's for you! Edward O'Connor, Esq.—a Protestant in the parish—two pounds."

" Long life to him !" cried a voice in the chapel.

" Amen !" said Father Phil; " I'm not ashamed to be clerk to so good a prayer."

Nicholas Fagan, £0 2s. 6d.

Young Nicholas Fagan, £0 5s. 0d. " Young Nick is better than ould Nick, you see."

Tim Doyle, £0 7s. 6d.

Owny Doyle, £1 0s. 0d. " Well done, Owny na Coppal— you deserve to prosper, for you make good use of your thrivings."

Simon Leary, £0 2s. 6d.; Bridget Murphy, £0 10s. 0d. " You ought to be ashamed o' yourself, Simon: a lone widow woman gives more than you."

*　　*　　*　　*　　*　　*　　*

Jude Moylan, £0 5s. 0d. " Very good, Judy, the women are behaving like gentlemen ; they'll have their reward in the next world."

Pat Finnerty, £0 8s. 4d. " I'm not sure if it is 8s. 4d. or 3s. 4d., for the figure is blotted, but I believe it is 8s. 4d."

" It was three and fourpince I gave your Reverence," said Pat from the crowd.

" Well, Pat, as I said eight and fourpence, you must not let me go back o' my word, so bring me five shillings next week."

" Sure, you wouldn't have me pay for a blot, sir ?"

" Yis, I would; that's the rule of backgammon, you know,
Pat. When I hit the mark, you pay for it."

Here his Reverence turned around, as if looking for some
one, and called out, " Rafferty ! Rafferty ! Rafferty ! Where
are you, Rafferty ?"

An old gray-headed man appeared, bearing a large plate,
and Father Phil continued—

"There now, be active—I'm sending him among you,
good people, and such as cannot give as much as you
would like to be read before your neighbors, give what little you can towards the repairs, and I will continue to read
out the names by way of encouragement to you—and
the next name I see is that of Squire Egan. Long life to
him !"

SQUIRE EGAN, £5 0s. 0d. " Squire Egan—five pounds
—listen to that—*a Protestant in the parish*—five pounds !
Faith, the Protestants will make you ashamed of yourselves if you don't take care."

Mrs. Flanagan, £2 0s. 0d. " Not her own parish, either
—a fine lady."

James Milligan of Roundtown, £1 0s. 0d. " And here I
must remark that the people of Roundtown have not been
backward in coming forward on this occasion. I have a
long list from Roundtown—I will read it separate." He
then proceeded at a great pace, jumbling the town and the
pounds and the people in the most extraordinary manner :
" James Milligan of Roundtown, one pound ; Darby Daly
of Roundtown, one pound ; Sam Finnegan of Roundtown,
one pound ; James Casey of Roundpound, one town ; Kit
Dwyer of Townpound, one round—pound, I mane ; Pat
Roundpound—Pounden, I mane—Pat Pounden a pound of
Poundtown also—there's an example for you !—

" But what are you about, Rafferty ? I don't like the
sound of that plate of yours—you are not a good gleaner—
go up first into the gallery there, where I see so many
good-looking bonnets—I suppose they will give something

to keep their bonnets out of the rain, for the wet will be into the gallery next Sunday if they don't. I think that is Kitty Crow I see, getting her bit of silver ready ; them ribbons of yours cost a thrifle, Kitty— Well, good Christians, here is more of the subscription for you."

Matthew Lavery, £0 2s. 6d. "He doesn't belong to Roundtown —Roundtown will be renowned in future ages for the support of the Church. Mark my words ! Roundtown will prosper from this day out—Roundtown will be a rising place."

Mark Hennessy, £0 2s. 6d.; Luke Clancy, £0 2s. 6d.; John Doolin, £0 2s. 6d. "One would think they had all agreed only to give two and sixpence apiece. And they comfortable men, too ! And look at their names—Matthew, Mark, Luke and John—the names of the blessed Evangelists, and only ten shillings among them. Oh, they are apostles not worthy the name—we'll call them the poor apostles from this out !" (Here a low laugh ran through the chapel.) "Do you hear that, Matthew, Mark, Luke and John ? Faith ! I can tell you that name will stick to you." (Here the laugh was louder.)

A voice, when the laugh subsided, exclaimed, " I'll make it ten shillin's, your Reverence."

"Who's that ?" said Father Phil.

"Hennessy, your Reverence."

" Very well, Mark. I suppose Matthew, Luke and John will follow your example ?"

" We will, your Reverence."

" Ha ! I thought you made a mistake ; we'll call you now the faithful apostles—and I think the change in your name is better than seven and sixpence apiece to you."

"I see you in the gallery there, Rafferty. What do you pass that well-dressed woman for ? thry back—Ha ! see that, she had her money ready if you only asked her for it —don't go by that other woman there— Oh, ho ! So you won't give anything, ma'am ? You ought to be ashamed

of yourself. There is a woman with an elegant sthraw
bonnet, and she won't give a farthing. Well now, afther
that, remember —I give it from the althar, that from this
day out sthraw bonnets pay fi'penny pieces."

Thomas Durfy, Esq., £1 0s. 0d. " It's not his parish,
and he's a brave gentleman."

Miss Fanny Dawson, £1 0s. 0d. " *A Protestant out of
the parish*, and a sweet young lady, God bless her! Oh,
faith, the Protestants is shaming you!"

Dennis Fannin, £0 7s. 6d. " Very good indeed, for a
working mason."

Jemmy Riley, £0 5s. 0d. "Not bad for a hedge car-
penther."

" I gave you ten, plaze your Reverence," shouted Jemmy; "and by the same token, you may remember it was
on the Nativity of the blessed Vargin, sir, I gave you the
second five shillin's."

" So you did, Jemmy," cried Father Phil; " I put a little
cross before it, to remind me of it; but I was in a hurry to
make a sick call when you gave it to me, and forgot it
afther: and indeed myself doesn't know what I did with
that same five shillings."

Here a pallid woman, who was kneeling near the rails of
the altar, uttered an impassioned blessing, and exclaimed,
" Oh, that was the very five shillings, I'm sure, you gave
to me that very day, to buy some little comforts for my
poor husband, who was dying in the fever!" and the poor
woman burst into loud sobs as she spoke.

A deep thrill of emotion ran through the flock as this ac-
cidental proof of their poor pastor's beneficence burst upon
them; and as an affectionate murmur began to rise above
the silence which that emotion produced, the burly Father
Philip blushed like a girl at this publication of his charity,
and even at the foot of that altar where he stood, felt
something like shame in being discovered in the commis-
sion of that virtue so highly commended by the Providence

to whose worship that altar was raised. He uttered a
hasty " Whisht, whisht !" and waved with his outstretched
hands his flock into silence.

In an instant one of those sudden changes so common to
an Irish assembly, and scarcely credible to a stranger, took
place. The multitude was hushed, the grotesque of the
subscription list had passed away and was forgotten, and
that same man and that same multitude stood in altered
relations—*they* were again a reverent flock, and *he* once
more a solemn pastor; the natural play of his nation's
mirthful sarcasm was absorbed in a moment in the sacred-
ness of his office ; and, with a solemnity befitting the
highest occasion, he placed his hands together before his
breast, and, raising his eyes to Heaven, he poured forth
his sweet voice, with a tone of the deepest devotion, in that
reverential call for prayer, " *Orate, fratres !*"

The sound of a multitude gently kneeling down followed,
like the soft breaking of a quiet sea on a sandy beach ; and
when Father Philip turned to the altar to pray, his pent-up
feelings found vent in tears, and while he prayed he wept.

I believe such scenes as this are of not unfrequent occurrence in Ireland—that country so long suffering, so much
maligned, and so little understood.

Oh, rulers of Ireland ! why have you not sooner learned
to *lead* that people by love, whom all your severity has
been unable to *drive ?*

A LITERARY NIGHTMARE.

MARK TWAIN.

Will the reader please to cast his eye over the following
verses, and see if he can discover anything harmful in them ?

" Conductor, when you receive a fare,
Punch in the presence of the passenjare !
A blue trip slip for an eight-cent fare,

A buff trip slip for a six-cent fare,
A pink trip slip for a three-cent fare,
Punch in the presence of the passenjare!

CHORUS.

Punch, brothers! punch with care!
Punch in the presence of the passenjare!"

I came across these jingling rhymes in a newspaper, a little while ago, and read them a couple of times. They took instant and entire possession of me. All through breakfast they went waltzing through my brain; and when, at last, I rolled up my napkin, I could not tell whether I had eaten anything or not. I had carefully laid out my day's work the day before—a thrilling tragedy in the novel which I am writing. I went to my den to begin my deed of blood. I took up my pen; but all I could get it to say was, "Punch in the presence of the passenjare." I fought hard for an hour, but it was useless. My head kept humming, "A blue trip slip for an eight-cent fare, a buff trip slip for a six-cent fare," and so on and so on, without peace or respite. The day's work was ruined—I could see that plainly enough. I gave up and drifted down town, and presently discovered that my feet were keeping time to that relentless jingle. When I could stand it no longer I altered my step. But it did no good; those rhymes accommodated themselves to the new step, and went on harassing me just as before. I returned home, and suffered all the afternoon; suffered all through an unconscious and unrefreshing dinner; suffered, and cried, and jingled all through the evening; went to bed, and rolled, tossed and jingled right along, the same as ever; got up at midnight frantic, and tried to read; but there was nothing visible upon the whirling page except "Punch! punch in the presence of the passenjare!" By sunrise I was out of my mind, and everybody marveled and was distressed at the idiotic burden of my ravings: "Punch! oh, punch! punch in the presence of the passenjare!"

Two days later, on Saturday morning, I arose, a totter-
ing wreck, and went forth to fulfill an engagement with a
valued friend, the Rev. Mr. ——, to walk to the Talcott
Tower, ten miles distant. He stared at me, but asked no
questions. We started. Mr. —— talked, talked, talked
—as is his wont. I said nothing; I heard nothing. At the
end of a mile, Mr. —— said:

"Mark, are you sick? I never saw a man look so haggard and worn and absent-minded. Say something; do!"

Drearily, without enthusiasm, I said: "Punch, brothers!
punch with care! Punch in the presence of the passenjare!"

My friend eyed me blankly, looked perplexed, then said:

"I do not think I get your drift, Mark. There does not
seem to be any relevancy in what you have said, certainly
nothing sad; and yet—maybe it was the way you *said* the
words—I never heard anything that sounded so pathetic.
What is—"

But I heard no more. I was already far away with my
pitiless, heart-breaking "blue trip slip for an eight-cent
fare, buff trip slip for a six-cent fare, pink trip slip for a
three-cent fare; punch in the presence of the passenjare."
I do not know what occurred during the other nine miles.
However, all of a sudden Mr. —— laid his hand on my
shoulder and shouted:

"Oh, wake up! wake up! wake up! Don't sleep all
day! Here we are at the Tower, man! I have talked
myself deaf and dumb and blind, and never got a response.
Just look at this magnificent autumn landscape! Look at
it! look at it! Feast your eyes on it! You have traveled;
you have seen boasted landscapes elsewhere. Come, now,
deliver an honest opinion. What do you say to this?"

I sighed wearily, and murmured:

"A buff trip slip for a six-cent fare, a pink trip slip for
a three-cent fare, punch in the presence of the passenjare."

Rev. Mr. —— stood there, very grave, full of concern,
apparently, and looked long at me; then he said:

" Mark, there is something about this that I cannot understand. Those are about the same words you said before ; there does not seem to be anything in them, and yet
they nearly break my heart when you say them. Punch
in the—how is it they go ?"

I began at the beginning and repeated all the lines. My
friend's face lighted with interest. He said :

" Why, what a captivating jingle it is ! It is almost
music. It flows along so nicely. I have nearly caught the
rhymes myself. Say them over just once more, and then
I'll have them, sure."

I said them over. Then Mr. —— said them. He made
one little mistake, which I corrected. The next time and
the next he got them right. Now a great burden seemed
to tumble from my shoulders. That torturing jingle departed out of my brain, and a grateful sense of rest and
peace descended upon me. I was light-hearted enough to
sing ; and I did sing for half an hour, straight along, as
we went jogging homeward. Then my freed tongue found
blessed speech again, and the pent talk of many a weary
hour began to gush and flow. It flowed on and on, joyously,
jubilantly, until the fountain was empty and dry. As I
wrung my friend's hand at parting, I said :

" Haven't we had a royal good time ! But now I remember, you haven't said a word for two hours. Come,
come, out with something !"

The Rev. Mr. —— turned a lack-lustre eye upon me,
drew a deep sigh, and said, without animation, without
apparent consciousness :

" Punch, brothers ! punch with care ! Punch in the
presence of the passenjare !"

A pang shot through me as I said to myself, " Poor fellow, poor fellow ! he has got it now."

I did not see Mr. —— for two or three days after that.
Then, on Tuesday evening, he staggered into my presence
and sank dejectedly into a seat. He was pale, worn ; he

was a wreck. He lifted his faded eyes to my face and said: "Ah, Mark, it was a ruinous investment that I made in those heartless rhymes. They have ridden me like a nightmare, day and night, hour after hour, to this very moment. Since I saw you I have suffered the torments of the lost. Saturday evening I had a sudden call by telegraph, and took the night train for Boston. The occasion was the death of a valued old friend, who had requested that I should preach his funeral sermon. I took my seat in the cars and set myself to framing the discourse. But I never got beyond the opening paragraph; for then the train started and the car-wheels began their ' clack-clack-clack-clack ! clack-clack-clack-clack !' and right away those odious rhymes fitted themselves to that accompaniment. For an hour I sat there and set a syllable of those rhymes to every separate and distinct clack the car-wheels made. Why, I was as fagged out then as if I had been chopping wood all day. My skull was splitting with headache. It seemed to me that I must go mad if I sat there any longer; so I undressed and went to bed. I stretched myself out in my berth, and—well, you know what the result was. The thing went right along, just the same. ' Clack-clack-clack, a blue trip slip, clack-clack-clack, for an eight-cent fare ; clack-clack-clack, a buff trip slip, clack-clack-clack, for a six-cent fare—and so on, and so on, and so on—*punch* in the presence of the passenjare !' Sleep ? Not a single wink ! I was almost a lunatic when I got to Boston. Don't ask me about the funeral. I did the best I could; but every solemn individual sentence was meshed and tangled and woven in and out with ' Punch, brothers ! punch with care ! punch in the presence of the passenjare.' And the most distressing thing was that my *delivery* dropped into the undulating rhythm of those pulsing rhymes, and I could actually catch absent-minded people nodding *time* to the swing of it with their stupid heads. And, Mark, you may believe it or not, but before I got through, the

entire assemblage were placidly bobbing their head in
solemn unison, mourners, undertaker, and all. The moment I had finished, I fled to the anteroom in a state bor-
dering on frenzy. Of course it would be my luck to find a
sorrowing and aged maiden aunt of the deceased there,
who had arrived from Springfield too late to get into the
church. She began to sob, and said :

" ' Oh, oh, he is gone, he is gone, and I didn't see him
before he died !'

" ' Yes !' I said, ' he *is* gone, he *is* gone, he *is* gone—oh,
will this suffering never cease ?'

" ' *You* loved him, then ! Oh, you too loved him !'

" ' Loved him ! Loved *who* ?'

" ' Why, my poor George ! my poor nephew !'

" ' Oh—*him* ! Yes—oh, yes, yes. Certainly—certainly.
Punch—punch—oh, this misery will kill me !'

" ' Bless you ! bless you, sir, for those sweet words ! *I*,
too, suffer in this dear loss. Were you present during his
last moments ?'

" ' Yes ! I—*whose* last moments ?'

" ' *His.* The dear departed's.'

" ' Yes ! Oh, yes—yes—*yes* ! I suppose so, I think so, *I*
don't know ! Oh, certainly—I was there—*I* was there !'

" ' Oh, what a privilege ! what a precious privilege.
And his last words—oh, tell me—tell me his last words !
What did he say ?'

" ' He said—he said—oh, my head, my head, my head !
He said—he said—he never said *any*thing but Punch,
punch, *punch* in the presence of the passenjare ! Oh, leave
me, madam ! In the name of all that is generous, leave me
to my madness, my misery, my despair !—a buff trip slip
for a six-cent fare, a pink trip slip for a three-cent fare—
endu-rance *can* no fur-ther go !—PUNCH in the presence of
the passenjare !' "

My friend's hopeless eyes rested on mine a pregnant
minute, and then he said impressively :

"Mark, you do not say anything. You do not offer me any hope. But, ah me, it is just as well—it is just as well. You could not do me any good. The time has long gone by when words could comfort me. Something tells me that my tongue is doomed to wag forever to the jigger of that remorseless jingle. There—there it is coming on me again: a blue trip slip for an eight-cent fare, a buff trip slip for a—"

Thus murmuring faint and fainter, my friend sank into a peaceful trance, and forgot his sufferings in a blessed respite.

How did I finally save him from the asylum? I took him to a neighboring university, and made him discharge the burden of his persecuting rhymes into the eager ears of the poor unthinking students. How is it with *them*, now? The result is too sad to tell. Why did I write this article? It was for a worthy, even a noble purpose. It was to warn you, reader, if you should come across those merciless rhymes, to avoid them—avoid them as you would a pestilence!

THE BIRTH OF IRELAND.

From the National Teacher's Monthly.

"With due condescension, I'd call your attention to what I shall
    mention of Erin so green,
And, without hesitation, I'll show how that nation became, of crea-
    tion, the gem and the queen.

"'Twas early one morning, without any warning, that Vanus was
    born in the beautiful Say;
And, by the same token, and sure 'twas provoking, her pinions
    were soaking, and wouldn't give play.

"Old Neptune, who knew her, began to pursue her, in order to
    woo her—the wicked old Jew—

And almost had caught her atop of the water—great Jupiter's
daughter!—which never would do.

"But Jove, the great janius, looked down and saw Vanus and
Neptune so heinous pursuing her wild,
And he spoke out in thunder he'd rend him asunder—and sure
'twas no wonder—for tazing his child.

"A star that was flying hard by him espying, he caught with
small trying and down let it snap;
It fell quick as winking on Neptune a-sinking, and gave him, I'm
thinking, a bit of a rap.

"*That star it was dryland, both lowland and highland, and formed
a sweet island, the land of my birth:*
Thus plain is the story that, sent down from glory, old Erin
asthore is the gem of the earth!

"Upon Erin nately jumped Vanus so stately, but fainted *kase*
lately so hard she was pressed;
Which much did bewilder, but, ere it had killed her, her father
distilled her a drop of the best.

"That sup was victorious; it made her feel glorious—a little up-
roarious, I fear it might prove—
So how can ye blame us that Ireland's so famous for drinking and
beauty, for fighting and love?"

THE IRISHMAN'S PANORAMA.

Kindness of MR. JAS. BURDETTE, Humorist and Dramatic Recitationist.

Ladies and Gintlemin: In the foreground over there
ye's 'll obsarve Vinegar Hill, an' should yer be goin' by
that way some day, yer moight be fatigued, an' if ye are
yer'll foind at the fut of the hill a nate little cot kept by·a
man named McCarty, who, by the way, is as foine a lad as
you'll mate in a day's march. I see by the hasp on the
door that McCarty is out, or I'd tak' yes in an' introduce
yes. A foine, ginerous, noble feller is this McCarty.

Shure an' if he had but the wan peratie he'd give yes the half of that, and phat's more, he'd thank ye for takin' it. (James, move the crank! Larry, music on the bag-pipes!)

Ladies and Gintlemin: We've now arrived at a beautiful spot, situated about twenty miles this side o' Limerick. To the left over there yer'll see a hut, by the side of which is sated a lady and gintleman; well, as I was goin' that way wan day I heard the following conversation betwixt him an' her. Says she to him: "James, it's a shame for yer to be tratin' me so; d'ye moind the toime yer used to come to me father's castle a-beggin'?" "Yer father's castle—*me?* Well, thin! ye could sthand on the outside of yer father's castle, an' stick yer arm down the chimney an' pick praties out of the pot, an' divil a partition betwixt you and the pigs but sthraw." (Move the crank, etc.)

Ladies an' Gintlemin: We have now arrived at the beautiful an' classical Lakes of Killarney. There's a curious legend connected wid dese lakes that I must relate to you. It is that every evenin' at four o'clock in the afternoon a beautiful swan is seen to make its appearance, an' while movin' transcendentally an' glidelessly along, ducks its head, skips under the water, an' you'll not see him till the next afternoon. (Turn the crank, etc.)

Ladies an' Gintlemin: We have now arrived at another beautiful spot, situated about thirteen and a half miles this side of Cork. This is a grate place, noted for sportsmin. Wanst, while sthoppin' over there at the hotel de Finney, the following tilt of a conversation occurred betwixt Mr. Muldooney, the waiter, and mesilf. I says to him says I, "Mully, old boy, will you have the kindness to fetch me the mustard?" and he was a long time bringin' it, so I opportuned him for kapin' me. An' says he to me, says he, "Mr. McCune" (that's me), "I notice that you take a grate dale of mustard wid your mate." "I do," says I. Says he, "I notice you take a blame sight of mate wid your mustard." (Move the crank, etc.)

Ladies an' Gintlemin : We now skhip acrost the broad Atlantic to a wonderful sphot in America, situated a few miles from Chinchinnatti, Ohoho, called the Falls of Niagara. While lingerin' here wan day I saw a young couple, evidently very sweet on aich other. Av coorse I tuk no notice of phat they were sayin', but I couldn't help listenin' to the followin' extraordinary conversation. Says he to her : " Isn't it wonderful to see that tremindous amount of water comin' down over that terrible precipice. " Yis, darlint," says she, " but wouldn't it be far more wonderful to see the same tremindous body of water a-goin' *up* that same precipice ?" (Move the crank, etc.)

MONEY MUSK.

BENJ. F. TAYLOR.

Abridged for Public Reading.

*   *   *   *   *   *

Ah, the buxom girls that helped the boys—
The nobler Helens of humbler Troys—
As they stripped the husks with rustling fold
From eight-rowed corn as yellow as gold,

By the candle-light in pumpkin bowls,
And the gleams that showed fantastic holes
In the quaint old lantern's tattooed tin,
From the hermit glim set up within ;

By the rarer light in girlish eyes
As dark as wells, or as blue as skies.
I hear the laugh when the ear is red,
I see the blush with the forfeit paid,

The cedar cakes with the ancient twist,
The cider cup that the girls have kissed.
And I see the fiddler through the dusk
As he twangs the ghost of "Money Musk!"

The boys and girls in a double row
Wait face to face till the magic bow
Shall whip the tune from the violin,
And the merry pulse of the feet begin.

MONEY MUSK.

In shirt of check, and tallowed hair,
The fiddler sits in the bulrush chair
Like Moses' basket stranded there
     On the brink of Father Nile.
He feels the fiddle's slender neck,
Picks out the note, with thrum and check;
And times the tune with nod and beck,
     And thinks it a weary while.
All ready! Now he gives the call,
Cries, "*Honor to the ladies!*" All
The jolly tides of laughter fall
     And ebb in a happy smile.

"*Begin.*" D-o-w-n comes the bow on every string,
"*First couple join right hands and swing!*"
As light as any blue-bird's wing
     "*Swing once and a half times round.*"
Whirls Mary Martin all in blue—
Calico gown and stockings new,
And tinted eyes that tell you true,
     Dance all to the dancing sound.

She flits about big Moses Brown,
Who holds her hands to keep her down
And thinks her hair a golden crown,
     And his heart turns over once!
His cheek with Mary's breath is wet,
It gives a second somerset!
He means to win the maiden yet,
     Alas, for the awkward dance!

"Your stoga boot has crushed my toe!"
"I'd rather dance with one-legged Joe!"
"You clumsy fellow!" "*Pass below!*"
     And the first pair dance apart.

Then " *Forward six !*" advance, retreat,
Like midges gay in sunbeam street
'Tis Money Musk by merry feet
        And the Money Musk by heart!

" *Three quarters round your partner swing !*"
" *Across the set !*"   The rafters ring,
The girls and boys have taken wing
        And have brought their roses out!
'Tis *Forward six !*" with rustic grace,
Ah, rarer far than—"*Swing to place !*"
Than golden clouds of old point-lace
        They bring the dance about.

Then clasping hands all—"*Right and left !*"
All swiftly weave the measure deft
Across the woof in loving weft,
        And the Money Musk is done !
Oh, dancers of the rustling husk,
Good night, sweet hearts, 'tis growing dusk,
Good night for aye to Money Musk,
        For the heavy march begun !

THE SHIP OF FAITH.

ANON.

A certain colored brother had been holding forth to his
little flock upon the ever-fruitful topic of *Faith*, and he
closed his exhortation about as follows :

My bruddren, ef yous gwine to git saved, you got to
git on board de Ship ob Faith.   I tell you, my bruddren,
dere ain't no odder way.   Dere ain't no gitten up de back
stairs, nor goin' 'cross lots ; you can't do dat away, my
bruddren, you got to git on board de Ship of Faith.   Once
'pon a time dere was a lot ob colored people, an' dey was
all gwine to de promised land.   Well, dey knowed dere want
no odder way for 'em to do but to git on board de Ship of

Faith. So dey all went down an' got on board, de ole gran-faders, an' de ole granmudders, an' de pickaninnies, an' all de res' ob 'em. Dey all got on board 'ceptin' one mons'us big feller, he said he's gwine to swim, *he* was. "W'y!" dey said, "you can't swim so fur like dat. It am a powerful long way to de promised land!" He said, "I kin swim anywhur, I kin. I git board no boat, no, 'deed!" Well, my bruddren, all dey could say to dat poor disluded man dey couldn't git him on board de Ship of Faith, so dey started off. De day was fair, de win' right; de sun shinin' and ev'ryt'ing b'utiful, an' dis big feller he pull off his close and plunge in de water. Well, he war a powerful swim-mer, dat man, 'deed he war; he war dat powerful he kep' right 'long side de boat all de time; he kep' a hollerin' out to de people on de boat, sayin': "What you doin' dere, you folks, brilin' away in de sun; you better come down heah in de water, nice an' cool down here." But dey said: "Man alive, you better come up here in dis boat while you got a chance." But he said, "No, indeedy! I git aboard no boat; I'm havin' plenty fun in de water." Well, bimeby, my bruddren, what you tink dat pore man seen? *A horrible, awful shark*, my bruddren; mouf wide open, teef more'n a foot long, ready to chaw dat pore man all up de minute he catch him. Well, when he seen dat shark he begun to git awful scared, an' he holler out to de folks on board de ship: "Take me on board, take me on board, quick!" But dey said: "No, indeed; you wouldn't come up here when you had an invite, you got to swim now."

He look over his shoulder an' he seen dat shark a-comin', an' he let hisself out. Fust it was de man an' den it was de shark, an' den it was de man again, dat away, my bruddren, *plum to de promised land.* Dat am de blessed troof I'm a tellin' you dis minute. But what do you t'ink was a-waitin' for him on de odder shore when he got dere? *A horrible, awful lion*, my bruddren, was a-stan'in'

dere on de shore, a-lashin' his sides wid his tail, an'
a-roarin' away fit to devour dat poor nigger de minit he
git on der shore. Well he *war* powerful scared den, he
don't know what he gwine to do. If he stay in de water
de shark eat him up; if he go on de shore de lion eat him
up; he dunno what to do. But he put his trust in de Lord,
an' went for de shore. Dat lion he give a fearful roar an'
bound for him; but, my bruddren, as sure as you 'live an'
breeve, dat horrible awful lion he jump clean ober dat pore
feller's head into de water; an' *de shark eat de lion*. But,
my bruddren, don't you put your trust in no sich circum-
stance; dat pore man he done git saved, but I tell you *de
Lord ain't a-gwine to furnish a lion for every nigger!*

PUP-PUP-POETRY.

PUNCH.

I have found a gig-gig-girl for my fuf-fuf-fair,
  I have found where the rattlesnakes bub-bub-breed;
Will you co-co-come, and I'll show you the bub-bub-bear,
  And the lions and tit-tit-tigers at fuf-fuf-feed.

I know where the co-co-cockatoo's song
  Makes mum-mum-melody through the sweet vale;
Where the mum-monkey's gig-gig-grin all the day long,
  Or gracefully swing by the tit-tail.

You shall pip-play, dear, some did-did delicate joke,
  With the bub bub-bear on the tit-tit-top of his pip-pip-pole;
But observe 'tis forbidden to pip-poke
  At the bub-bub-bear with your pip pip-pink pip-pip-pip-parasol.

You shall see the huge elephant pip-pip-play;
  You shall gig-gig-gaze on the stit-stit-ately raccoon,
And then, did-dear, together we'll stray
  To the cage of the bub-bub-blue-faced bab-bab-baboon.

You wished (I r-r-remembered it well,
  And I lul-lul-loved you the m-m-more for the wish)
To witness the bub-bub-beautiful pip-pip-pelican
  Swallow the l-l-live little fuf-fuf-fish.

A SENATOR ENTANGLED.

JAMES DE MILLE.

From The Dodge Club.

Our Senator was a man who by mere force of character, apart from the adventitious aids of culture and refinement, had attained wealth and position. He found it agreeable —as so many other Americans have done—to take a trip abroad.

He chanced to be in Florence during the recent struggle for Italian independence. His friend, the Minister, took him to the houses of the leaders of society, and introduced him as an eminent American statesman and member of the Senate.

Could any recommendation be equal to that? Republicanism ran high. America was synonymous with the Promised Land. To be a statesman in America was as great a dignity as to be prince in any empire on earth.

So if the Florentines received the Senator with boundless hospitality, it was because they admired his country, and reverenced his dignity. They liked to consider the presence of the American Minister and Senator as an expression of the good-will of the American government. They were determined to lionize him. It was a new sensation to the Senator.

For two or three days he was the subject of an eager contest among all the leaders of society. At length there appeared upon the scene the great Victrix in a thousand contests such as these. The others fell back discomfited, and the Senator became her prey.

The Countess di Nottinero was not exactly a Recamier, but she was a remarkably brilliant woman, and the acknowledged leader of the liberal part of Florentine society.

She was generally known as *La Cica*, a nickname given by her enemies, though what " Cica " meant no one could tell exactly.

La Cica did her part marvelously well. She did not speak the best English in the world, yet that could not account for all the singular remarks which she made. Still less could it account for the tender interest of her manner. She had remarkably bright eyes. Why wandered those eyes so often to his, and why did they beam with such devotion—beaming for a moment only to fall in sweet, innocent confusion? *La Cica* had the most fascinating manners, yet they were often perplexing to the Senator's soul. The little offices which she required of him did not appear, in his matter-of-fact eyes, as strictly prudent. The innate gallantry which he possessed carried him bravely along through much that was bewildering to his nerves. Yet he was often in danger of running away in terror.

" The Countess," he thought, " is a most remarkable fine woman; but she does use her eyes uncommon, and I do wish she wouldn't be quite so demonstrative."

The good Senator had never before encountered a thorough woman of the world, and was as ignorant as a child of the innumerable little harmless arts by which the power of such a one is extended and secured. At last the Senator came to this conclusion—*La Cica* was desperately in love with him.

She appeared to be a widow. At least, she had no husband that he had ever seen. Now if the poor *Cica* was hopelessly in love, it must be stopped at once. But let it be done delicately, not abruptly.

One evening they walked on the balcony of *La Cica's* noble residence. She was sentimental, devoted, charming.

The conversation of a fascinating woman does not sound so well when reported as it is when uttered. Her power is in her tone, her glance, her manner. Who can catch the evanescent beauty of her expression or the deep tenderness of her well-modulated voice? who indeed?   .

" Does ze scene please you, my Senator ?"

" Very much indeed."

" Youar countrymen haf tol me zey would like to stay here alloway."

" It is a beautiful place."

" Did you aiver see anythin' moaire loafely ?" And the Countess looked full in his face.

" Never," said the Senator, earnestly. The next instant he blushed. He nad been betrayed into a compliment.

The Countess sighed.

" Helas! my Senator, that it is not pairmitted to moartals to 'sociate as zey would laike."

" ' Your Senator,' " thought the gentleman thus addressed; "how fond, how tender—poor thing! poor thing!"

" I wish that Italy was nearer to the States," said he.

" How I adamiar youar style of mind, so differente from ze Italiana! You are so strong.—so nobile. Yet would I laike to see moar of ze poetic in you."

" I always loved poetry, marm," said the Senator, desperately.

" Ah—good—nais—eccelente. I am plees at zat," cried the Countess, with much animation. " You would loafe it moar eef you knew Italiano. Your langua ees not sufficiente musicale for poatry."

" It is not so soft a language as the Italian."

" Ah—no—not so soft. Very well. And what theenka you of ze Italiano ?"

" The sweetest language I ever heard in all my born days."

" Ah, now—you hev not heard much of ze Italiano, my Senator."

" I have heard you speak often," said the Senator, naïvely.

" Ah, you compliment! I sot you was aboove flattera."

And the Countess playfully tapped his arm with her little fan.

" What Ingelis poet do you loafe best ?"

" Poet! English poet ?" said the Senator, with some

surprise. "Oh—why, marm, I think Watts is about the best of tho lot!"

"Watt? Was he a poet? I did not know zat. He who invented ze stim-injaine? And yet, if he was a poet, it is naturale zat you loafe him best."

"Steam-engine? Oh, no! This one was a minister."

"A meeneestaire? Ah! an abbé? I know him not. Yet I haf read mos of all youar poets."

"He made up hymns, marm, and psalms—for instance, 'Watts's Divine Hymns and Spiritual Songs.'"

"Songs? Spirituelle? Ah, I mus at once procuaire ze works of Watt, which was favorit poet of my Senator."

"A lady of such intelligence as you would like the poet Watts," said the Senator, firmly. "He is the best known by far of all our poets."

"What! better zan Sakespeare, Milton, Bairon? You mucu surprass me."

"Better known and better loved than the whole lot. Why, his poetry is known by heart through all England and America."

"Merciful Heaven! what you tell me? ees eet possbl? An' yet he is not known here efen by name. It would please me mooch, my Senator, to haire you make one quotatione. Know you Watt? Tell to me some words of his which I may remembaire."

"I have a shocking bad memory."

"Bad memora! Oh, but you remember somethin', zis mos' beaut'ful charm nait—you haf a nobile soul—you mus' be affecta by beauty—by ze ideal. Make for a me one quotatione."

And she rested her little hand on the Senator's arm, and looked up imploringly in his face.

The Senator looked foolish. He felt even more so. Here was a beautiful woman, by act and look showing a tender interest in him. Perplexing—but very flattering, after all. So he replied—

" You will not let me refuse you anything."

" Aha! you are very willing to refuse. It is difficulty for me to excitaire youar regards. You are filled with the grands ideas. But come—will you spik for me some from your favorit Watt ?"

" Well, if you wish it so much," said the Senator, kindly; and he hesitated.

" Ah! I do wis it so much !"

' Ehem !"

"Begin," said the Countess. " Behold me. I listen. I hear every sin, and will remembaire it forava."

The only thing that the Senator could think of was a verse which had been running in his head for the last few days, its measured rhythm keeping time with every occupation :

" ' My willing soul would stay—' "

"Stop one moment," said the Countess. " I weesh to learn it from you ;" and she looked fondly and tenderly up, but instantly dropped her eyes.

" ' Ma willina sol wooda sta—' "

" ' In such a frame as this,' " prompted the Senator.

" ' Een socha framas zees.' Wait—' Ma willina sol wooda sta in soocha frama zees.' Ah, appropriat ! but could I hope zat you were true to zose lines, my Senator ? Well ?"

" ' And sit and sing herself away,' " said the Senator, in a faltering voice, and breaking out into a cold perspiration for fear of committing himself by such uncommonly strong language.

" ' Ansit ansin hassaf awai,' " repeated the Countess, her face lighting up with a sweetly conscious expression.

The Senator paused.

" Well ?"

" I—ehem ! I forget."

" Forget ? Impossible !"

" I do, really."

" Ah, now ! Forget ! I see by youar face—you desave. Say on."

The Countess again gently touched his arm with both of her little hands, and held it as though she would clasp it.

"Have you fear? Ah, cruel!"

The Senator turned pale, but, finding refusal impossible, boldly finished:

"'To everlasting bliss '—there!"

"'To affarlastin' blees thar.' Stop. I repeat it all: 'Ma willina sol wooda sta in socha framas zees, ausit ansin hassaf' awai to affarlastin blees thar.' Am I right!"

"Yes," said the Senator, meekly.

"I knew you war a poetic sola," said the Countess, confidingly. "You are honesto—true—you cannot desave. When you spik I can beliv you. Ah, my Senator! an you can spik zis poetry!—at soch a taime! I nefare knew befoare zat you were so impassione!—an' you air so artaful! You breeng ze confersazione to beauty—to poatry—to ze poet Watt—so you may spik verses mos impassione! Ah! what do you mean? Santissima madre! how I wish you spik Italiano."

The Countess drew nearer to him, but her approach only deepened his perplexity.

"How that poor thing does love me!" sighed the Senator. "Law bless it! she can't help it—can't help it nohow. She is a goner; and what can I do? I'll have to leave Florence."

The Countess was standing close beside him in a tender mood waiting for him to break the silence. How could he? He had been uttering words which sounded to her like love; and she—"a widow! a widow! a widow! wretched man that I am!"

There was a pause. The longer it lasted the more awkward the Senator felt. What upon earth was he to do or say? What business had he to go and quote poetry to widows? What an old fool he must be! But the Countess was very far from feeling awkward. Assuming an elegant attitude she looked up, her face expressing the tenderest solicitude.

" What ails my Senator ?"

" Why, the fact is, marm—I feel sad—at leaving Florence. I must go shortly. My wife has written summoning me home. The children are down with the measles."

O base fabrication ! O false Senator ! There wasn't a word of truth in that remark. You spoke so because you wished *La Cica* to know that you had a wife and family. Yet it was very badly done.

La Cica changed neither her attitude nor her expression. Evidently the existence of his wife and the melancholy situation of his unfortunate children awakened no sympathy.

" But, my Senator, did you not say you wooda seeng yoursellef away to affarlasteen belees ?"

" Oh, marm, it was a quotation—only a quotation."

But at this critical juncture the conversation was broken up by the arrival of a number of ladies and gentlemen.

CHRISTMAS-NIGHT IN THE QUARTERS.

IRWIN RUSSELL.
From Scribner's Monthly.
ABRIDGED FOR PUBLIC READING.

When merry Christmas-day is done,
And Christmas-night is just begun ;
While clouds in slow procession drift
To wish the moon-man " Christmas gift,"
Yet linger overhead, to know
What causes all the stir below ;
At Uncle Johnny Booker's ball
The darkeys hold high carnival.

    *   *   *   *   *   *

Original in act and thought,
Because unlearnèd and untaught,

Observe them at their Christmas party.
How unrestrained their mirth—how hearty!
How many things they say and do,
That never would occur to you!
See Brudder Brown—whose saving grace
Would sanctify a quarter-race—
Out on the crowded floor advance,
To "beg a blessin' on dis dance."

Oh, Mahsr! let dis gath'rin' fin' a blessin' in yo sight!
Don't jedge us hard for what we does—you know it's Chrismus
      night;
An' all de balunce ob de yeah we does as right's we kin—
Ef dancin's wrong—oh, Mahsr! let de time excuse de sin!

We labors in de vineya'd—workin' hard, an' workin' true—
Now, shorely you won't notus, ef we eats a grape or two,
An' takes a leetle holiday—a leetle restin'-spell—
Bekase, nex' week, we'll start in fresh, an' labor twicet as well.

Remember, Mahsr—min' dis, now—de sinfulness ob sin
Is 'pendin' 'pon de sperrit what we goes an' does it in:
An' in a righchis frame ob min' we's gwine to dance an' sing;
A-feelin' like King David, when he cut de pigeon-wing.

It seems to me—indeed it do—I mebbe mout be wrong—
That people raly *ought* to dance when Chrismus comes along;
Des dance bekase dey's happy—like de birds hops in de trees:
De pine-top fiddle soundin' to de bowin' ob de breeze.

We has no ark to dance afore, like Isrul's prophet king;
We has no harp to soun' de chords, to holp us out to sing;
But 'cordin' to de gif's we has we does de bes' we knows—
An' folks don't 'spise de vi'let-flow'r bekase it ain't de rose.

You bless us, please sah, eben ef we's doin' wrong to-night;
Kase den we'll need de blessin' more 'n ef we's doin' right;
An' let de blessin' stay wid us, untell we comes to die,
An' goes to keep our Chrismus wid dem sheriffs in de sky!

Yes, tell dem preshis anjuls we's a-gwine to jine 'em soon:
Our voices we's a-trainin' for to sing de glory tune;
We's ready when you wants us, an' it ain't no matter when—
Oh, Mahsr! call yo' chillen soon, an' take 'em home! Amen.

The rev'rend man is scarcely through,
When all the noise begins anew,
And with such force assaults the ears,
That through the din one hardly hears
Old Fiddling Josey "sound his A"—
Correct the pitch—begin to play—
Stop, satisfied—then, with the bow,
Rap out the signal dancers know :

Git yo' pardners, fus kwattilion!
Stomp yo' feet, an' raise 'em high;
Tune is: " Oh! dat water-million !
Gwine to git to home bime-bye."
S'lute yo' pardners! scrape perlitely—
Don't be bumpin' gin de res'—
Balance all! now, step out rightly;
Alluz dance yo' lebbel bes'.
Fo'wa'd foah!—whoop up, niggers !
Back ag'in!—don't be so slow—
Swing cornahs!—min' de figgers :
When I holler, den yo' go.
Top ladies cross ober!
Hol' on, till I takes a dram—
Gemmen solo!—yes, I's sober—
Kaint say how de fiddle am—
Hands around!—hol' up yo' faces,
Don't be lookin' at yo' feet !
Swing yo' pardners to yo' places!
Dat's de way—dat's hard to beat.
Sides fo'w'd!—when you's ready—
Make a bow as low's you kin !
Swing acrost wid opp'site lady!
Now we'll let you swap ag'in :
Ladies change!—shet up dat talkin';
Do yo' talkin arter while—
Right an' lef'!—don't want no walkin'—
Make yo' steps an' show yo' style !
*   *   *   *   *

So wears the night: and wears so fast,
All wonder when they find it passed,

And hear the signal sound, to go,
From what few cocks are left to crow.
Then one and all you hear them shout:
"Hi! Booker! fotch de banjo out,
An' gib us *one* song 'fore we goes—
One ob de berry bes' you knows!"
Responding to the welcome call,
He takes the banjo from the wall,
And tunes the strings with skill and care—
Then strikes them with a master's air ;
And tells in melody and rhyme,
This legend of the olden time :

Go 'way fiddle !—folks is tired o' hearin' you a-squarkin'
Keep silence for yo' betters—don't you heah de banjo talkin' ?
About de 'possum's tail she's gwine to lecter—ladies, listen !—
About de ha'r what isn't dar, an' why de ha'r is missin' :

" Dar's gwine to be a oberflow," said Noah, lookin' solemn—
For Noah tuk the " Herald," an' he read de ribber column—
An' so he sot his hands to work a-cl'arin' timber-patches,
An' 'lowed he's gwine to build a boat to beat de steamah
      " Natchez."

Ol' Noah kep' a-nailin', an' a-chippin', an' a-sawin' ;
An' all the wicked neighbors kep' a-laughin' an' a-pshawin' ;
But Noah didn't min' 'em—knowin' whut wuz gwine to happen:
An' forty days an' forty nights de rain it kep' a-drappin'.

Now, Noah had done cotched a lot ob ebry sort o' beas'es—
Ob all de shows a-trabbelin', it beat 'em all to pieces!
He had a Morgan colt, an' sebral head o' Jarsey cattle—
An' druv 'em 'board de Ark as soon's he heered de thunder rattle.

Den sech anoder fall ob rain !—it come so awful hebby,
De ribber riz immejitly, an' busted troo de lebbee ;
De people all wuz drownded out—'cep' Noah an' de critters,
An' men he'd hired to work de boat—an' one to mix de bitters.

De Ark she kep' a-sailin', an' a-sailin', *an'* a-sailin' ;
De lion got his dander up, an' like to bruk de pailin'—
De sarpints hissed—de painters yelled—tell, what wid all de fussin'
You c'u'dn't hardly heah de mate a-bossin' 'roun' an' cussin'.

Now, Ham, de only nigger whut wuz runnin' on de packet,
Got lonesome in de barber-shop, an' c'u'dn't stan' de racket;
An' so, for to amuse he-se'f, he steamed some wood an' bent it,
An' soon he had a banjo made—de fust dat wuz invented.

He wet de ledder, stretched it on; made bridge, an' screws, an'
    apron;
An' fitted in a proper neck—'twuz berry long an' tap'rin';
He tuk some tin, an' twisted him a thimble for to ring it;
An' den de mighty question riz : how wuz he gwine to string it?

De 'possum had as fine a tail as dis dat I's a-singin';
De ha'rs so long, an' thick, an' strong—des fit for banjo-stringin';
Dat nigger shaved 'em off as short as wash-day dinner graces ;
An' sorted ob 'em by de size, frum little E's to basses.

He strung her, tuned her, struck a jig—'twuz " Nebber min' de
    wedder "—
She soun' like forty-lebben bands a-playin' all togedder ;
Some went to pattin'; some to dancin'; Noan called de figgers—
An' Ham he sot an' knocked de tune, de happiest ob niggers!

Now, sence dat time—it's mighty strange—dere's not de slightes'
    showin'
Ob any ha'r at all upon de 'possum's tail a-growin';
An' curi's, too—dat nigger's ways : his people nebber los' 'em—
For whar you finds de nigger—dar's de banjo an' de 'possum!

    The night is spent; and as the day
    Throws up the first faint flash of gray,
    The guests pursue their homeward way;
    And through the field beyond the gin,
    Just as the stars are going in,
    See Santa Claus departing—grieving—
    His own dear Land of Cotton leaving.
    His work is done—he fain would rest,
    Where people know and love him best—
    He pauses—listens—looks about—
    But go he must: his pass is out;
    So, coughing down the rising tears,
    He climbs the fence and disappears

And thus observes a colored youth—
(The common sentiment, in sooth) :
" Oh ! what a blessing 'tw'u'd ha' been
Ef Santy had been born a twin !
We'd hab two Christmuses a yeah—
Or p'r'aps *one* brudder'd *settle* heah !"

A LOVE SONG.

ANON.

Och, Nora, so swate, an' so purty, the darlint !
    Her cheeks are like pinks shinin' out av the snow ;
An' her chin—och, my heart, the dimple that's in it !—
    An' eyes that say yis when her lips utter no.

Her form it is iligant, trim like, an' slinder ;
    An' look at the flowers that are harkin' all 'round
To hear is she comin', wid kisses so tinder
    To give her white fut as it touches the ground !

An' oft do I mind the fust hour of our meetin'—
    The baste of a dog, he had frighted her so ;
She sprang to my arms, her poor heart wildly beatin'
    Wid fear ; but i' faith, not a bit did I know

What it was ailin' mine—sich a stir an' commotion
    Inside of my chist, where her purty head lay,
While my breath came in whirls, like the breath of the ocean,
    An' tripped up the words I was wantin' to say.

An' here am I waitin' an hour in the gloamin
    Wid cruel lone spells sinkin' down in my heart ;
Hist ! that is hersilf now, so craftily comin'
    To tase a poor lad wid her guile an' her art.

But ye'll not git away, sure, my beautiful daisy ;
    Rest here in the arms that are lovin' an' strong.
Kape still now, mavourneen, ye'd betther be aisy—
    Some other big dog might be comin' along.

THE STEAMBOAT RACE.

From the " Gilded Age."

MARK TWAIN.

Presently the pilot said :

" By George, yonder comes the Amaranth !"

A spark appeared close to the water, several miles down the river. The pilot took his glass and looked at it steadily for a moment, and said, chiefly to himself: " It can't be the Blue Wing; she couldn't pick us up this way. It's the Amaranth, sure."

He bent over a speaking-tube and said :

" Who's on watch down there ?"

A hollow, inhuman voice mumbled up through the tube in answer :

" I am—second engineer."

" Good ! you want to stir your stumps, now, Harry ; the Amaranth's just turned the point, and she's just a humping herself, too !"

The pilot took hold of a rope that stretched out forward, jerked it twice, and two mellow strokes of the big bell responded.

A voice on deck shouted :

" Stand by, down there, with that larboard lead !"

" No, I don't want the lead," said the pilot ; " I want *you.* Roust out the old man—tell him the Amaranth's coming. And go and call Jim—tell *him.*"

" Aye! aye ! sir."

The " old man " was the captain. He is always called so on steamboats and ships. " Jim " was the other pilot. Within two minutes both these men were flying up the pilot-house stairway, three steps at a jump. Jim was in his shirt sleeves, with his coat and vest on his arm. He said :

" I was just turning in. Where's the glass ?"

He took it and looked :

" Don't appear to be any night hawk on the jack's staff;
it's the Amaranth, dead sure !"

The captain took a good long look and only said :

" Damnation !"

George Davis, the pilot on watch, shouted to the night
watchman on deck :

" How's she loaded ?"

" Two inches by the head, sir."

" 'Taint enough !"

The captain shouted, now :

" Call the mate. Tell him to call all hands and get a lot
of that sugar forrard—put her ten inches by the head.
Lively, now !"

" Aye ! aye ! sir !"

A riot of shouting and trampling floated up from below,
presently, and the uneasy steering of the boat soon showed
that she was getting " down by the head."

The three men in the pilot-house began to talk in short,
sharp sentences, low and earnestly. As their excitement
rose, their voices went down. As fast as one of them put
down the spy-glass, another took it up—but always with
a studied air of calmness. Each time the verdict was :

" She's a-gaining !"

The captain spoke through the tube :

" What steam are you carrying ?"

" A hundred and forty-two, sir ! but she's getting hotter
and hotter all the time."

The boat was straining, and groaning and quivering,
like a monster in pain. Both pilots were at work, now, one
on each side of the wheel, with their coats and vests off,
their bosoms and collars wide open, and the perspiration
flowing down their faces. They were holding the boat so
close to the shore that the willows swept the guards almost from stem to stern.

" Stand by !" whispered George.

" All ready ! " said Jim under his breath.

" Let her come !"

The boat sprang away from the bank like a deer, and darted in a long diagonal toward the other shore. She closed in again and thrashed her fierce way along the willows as before. The captain put down the glass :

" Lord, how she walks up on us! I do hate to be beat !"

The Amaranth was within three hundred yards of the Boreas, and still gaining. The "old man" spoke through the tube :

" What is she carrying now ?"

" A hundred and sixty-five, sir."

" How's your wood ?"

" Pine all out, cypress half gone—eating up cotton wood like pie !"

" Break into that rosin on the main deck ! pile it in—the boat can pay for it !"

Soon the boat was plunging and quivering and screaming more madly than ever. But the Amaranth's head was almost abreast the Boreas' stern.

" How's your steam now, Harry ?"

" Hundred and eighty-two, sir."

" Break up the casks of bacon in the forrard hold ! Pile it in ! Levy on that turpentine in the fantail—drench every stick of wood with it !"

The boat was a moving earthquake by this time.

" How is she now ?"

" A hundred and ninety-six and still a-swelling !—water below the middle gauge cocks !—carrying every pound she can stand !—nigger roosting on the safety-valve !"

" Good ! How's your draught ?"

" Bully ! Every time a nigger heaves a stick of wood into the furnace he goes out the chimney with it !"

The Amaranth drew steadily up till her jack staff breasted the Boreas' wheel house—climbed along inch by inch till her chimneys breasted it.

" Jim," said George, looking straight ahead, watching

the slightest yawing of the boat and promptly meeting it with the wheel, " how'll it do to try Murderer's Chute ?"

" Well, it's—it's taking chances. How was the cotton wood stump on the false point below Boardman's Island this morning ?"

" Water just touching the roots."

" Well, it's pretty close work. That gives six feet scant in the head of Murderer's Chute. We can just barely rub through if we hit it exactly right. But it's worth trying. *She* don't dare tackle it," meaning the Amaranth.

In another instant the Boreas plunged into what seemed a crooked creek, and the lights of the Amaranth were shut out in a moment. Not a whisper was uttered, now, but the three men stared ahead into the shadows, and two of them spun the wheel back and forth with anxious watchfulness, while the steamer tore along. The Chute seemed to come to an end every fifty yards, but always opened out in time. Now the head of it was at hand. George tapped the big bell three times; two leadsmen sprang to their posts, and in a moment their weird cries rose on the night air and were caught up and repeated by two men on the upper deck :

" No-o bottom !"

" Deep four !"

" Half three !"

" Quarter three !"

" Mark under water three !"

" Half twain !"

" Quarter twain !—"

Davis pulled a couple of ropes, there was a jingling of small bells far below, the boat's speed slackened, and the pent steam began to whistle and the gauge cocks to scream :

" By the mark twain !"

" Quarter her—er—less twain !"

" Eight *and* a half !"

" Eight feet !"

" Seven an' a—half!—"

Another jingling of little bells and the wheels ceased turning altogether. The whistling of the steam was something frightful now; it almost drowned all other noises.

" Stand by to meet her !"

George had the wheel hard down and was standing on a spoke.

" All ready !"

The boat hesitated, seemed to hold her breath—as did the captain and pilots—and then she began to fall away to starboard, and every eye lighted :

"*Now* then! meet her! meet her! snatch her!" The wheel flew to port so fast that the spokes blended into a spider web, the swing of the boat subsided; she steadied herself.

" Seven feet !"

"Sev—six and a *half!*"

" *Six* feet ! Six f——"

Bang! She hit the bottom ! George shouted through the tube :

" Spread her wide open ! *Whale* it at her !"

The escape pipes belched snowy pillars of steam aloft, the boat groaned and surged and trembled, and slid over into—

" Mark twain !"

" Quarter her !"

Tap ! tap ! tap ! (to signify " lay in the leads.")

And away she went, flying up the willow shore with the whole silver sea of the Mississippi stretching abroad on every hand, and, *no* Amaranth in sight.

THE SWELL.

GEORGE W. KYLE.

I say ! I wonder why fellahs ever wide in horse-cars ? I've been twying all day to think why fellahs ever do it, weally ! I know some fellahs that are in business, down

town, you know—C. B. Jones, cotton dealer; Smith Brothers, woolen goods; Bwown & Company, stock bwokers
and that sort of thing, you know—who say they do it every
day. If I was to do it every day, my funeral would come
off in about a week. 'Pon my soul, it would. I wode in a
horse-car one day. Did it for a lark. Made a bet I would
wide in a horse-car, 'pon my soul, I did. So I went out on
the pavement before the club-house and called one. I said,
" Horse-car! horse-car!" but not one of 'em stopped,
weally! Then I saw that fellahs wun after them—played
tag with them, you know, as the dweadful little girls do
when school is coming out. And sometimes they caught
the cars—ah—and sometimes they did not. So I wun after
one, I did weally, and I caught it. I was out of breath,
you know, and a fellah on the platform—a conductor
fellah—poked me in the back and said, " Come! move up!
make room for this lady!" Ah—by Jove he did, you
know! I looked for the lady so (*eye-glass business*), but
I could see no lady, and I said so. There was a female
person behind me, with large market-basket, cwowded
with ah—vegetables and such dweadful stuff—and another
person with a bundle and another with a baby, you know.
The person with the basket prodded me in the back with
it, and I said to the conductor fellah, said I, " Where shall
I sit down? I—ah—I don't see any seat, you know."
(*Eye-glass business.*) " The seats seem to be occupied by
persons, conductor," said I. " Where shall I sit?"

He was wude, very wude, indeed, and he said, " You
can sit on your thumb if you have a mind to." And when
I wemonstrated with him upon the impwopwiety of telling
a gentleman to sit on his thumb, he told me to go to
thunder. " Go to thunder!" he did, indeed. After a while
one of the persons got out and I sat down; it was vewy
disagweeable! Opposite me there were several persons
belonging to the labowing classes, with what I pwesume
to be lime on their boots; and tin kettles which they car-

ried for some mysterious purpose in their hands. There
was a person with a large basket, and a colored person.
Next to me there sat a fellah that had been eating onions !
'Twas vewy offensive! I couldn't stand it! No fellah
could, you know. I had heard that if any one in a car was
annoyed by a fellah-passenger he should weport it to the
conductor. So I said, " Conductor ! put this person out of
tne car ! he annoys me vewy much. He has been eating
onions." But the conductor fellah only laughed. He did,
indeed ! And the fellah that had been eating onions said,
" Hang yer impidence, what do ye mean by that ?" " It's
extwemely disagweeable, you know, to sit near one who
has been eating onions," said I. " I think you ought to
resign, get out, you know." And then, though I'm sure I
spoke in the most wespectfully manner, he put his fist
under my nose and wemarked, " You'll eat that, hang you,
in a minute !" he did indeed. And a fellah opposite said,
" Put a head on him, Jim !" I suppose from his tone that
it was some colloquial expwession of the lower orders, re-
ferring to a personal attack. It was vewy disagweeable,
indeed. I don't see why any fellah ever wides in the horse-
cars. But I didn't want a wow, you know. A fellah is
apt to get a black eye, and a black eye spoils one's ap-
peawance, don't you think ? So I said, " Beg pardon, I'm
swre." The fellah said, " Oh, hang you !" he did, indeed.
He was a vewy ill-bred person. And all this time the car
kept stopping and more persons of the lower orders kept
petting on. A very dweadful woman with a vewy dweadful baby stood right before me, intercepting my view of
the street; and the baby had an orange in one hand
and some candy in the other. And I was wondering why
persons of the lower classes were allowed to have such
dirty babies, and why Bergh or some one didn't interfere,
you know, when, before I knew what she was doing, that
dweadful woman sat that dweadful baby wight down on
my lap ! She did, indeed. And it took hold of my shirt

bosom with one of its sticky hands and took my eye-glass
away with the other, and upon my honor, I'm quite lost
without my eye-glass. "You'll have to kape him till I
find me money," said the woman. "Weally!" said I,
"I'm not a nursery-maid ma'am." Then the people about
me laughed, they did, indeed. I could not endure it. I
jumped up and dwopped the baby in the straw. "Stop
the car, conductor," said I, "stop the car." What do you
suppose he said? "Hurry up now, be lively, be lively,
don't keep me waiting all day!" And I was about to
wemonstrate with him upon the impwopwiety of speaking
so to a gentleman, when he pushed me off the car. That
was the only time I ever wode in a horse-car. I wonder
why fellahs ever do wide in horse-cars? I should think
they would pwefer cabs, you know.

THE LITTLE STOW-AWAY.

ANON.

Abridged for Public Reading.

*   *   *   "Would ye like to hear about it?"

I eagerly assent; and the narrator, knocking the ashes
out of his pipe, folds his brawny arms upon the top of the
rail, and commences as follows:

"'Bout three years ago, afore I got this berth as I'm in
now, I was second engineer aboard a Liverpool steamer
bound for New York. There'd been a lot of extra cargo
sent down just at the last minute, and we'd had no end of
a job stowin' it away, and that ran us late o' startin'; so
that, altogether, you may think, the cap'n warn't in the
sweetest temper in the world, nor the mate neither; as for
the chief-engineer, he was an easy-goin' sort of a chap, as
nothing on earth could put out. But on the mornin' of the
third day out from Liverpool, he cum down to me in a pre-

cious hurry, lookin' as if somethin' had put him out pretty considerably.

" 'Tom,' says he, 'what d'ye think? Blest if we ain't found a stow-away.' (That's the name, you know, sir, as we gives to chaps as hide theirselves aboard outward-bound vessels, and gets carried out unbeknown to everybody.)

" 'The dickens you have!' says I. 'Who is he, and where did you find him?'

" ' Well, we found him stowed away among the casks for'ard; and ten to one we'd never ha' twigged him at all, if the skipper's dog hadn't sniffed him out and begun barkin'. Such a nice little mite as he is, too! I could ha' most put him in my baccy-pouch, poor little beggar! but he look to be a good-plucked un for all that.'

" I didn't wait to hear no more, but up on deck like a sky-rocket: and there I did see a sight, and no mistake. Every man-Jack o' the crew, and what few passengers we had aboard, was all in a ring on the fo'c'stle, and in the middle was the fust-mate, lookin' as black as thunder. Right in front of him, looking a reg'lar mite among them big fellers, was a little bit o' a lad not ten year old—ragged as a scare-crow, but with bright, curly hair, and a bonnie little face o' his own, it it hadn't been so woful thin and pale. But, bless your soul! to see the way that little chap held his head up, and looked about him, you'd ha' thought the whole ship belonged to him. The mate was a great hulkin' black-bearded feller, with a look that 'ud ha' frightened a horse, and a voice fit to make one jump through a key-hole; but the young un warn't a bit afeard —he stood straight up, and looked him full in the face with them bright, clear eyes o' his'n, for all the world as if he was Prince Halferd himself. Folk did say arterwards" —lowering his voice to a whisper—" as how he comed o' better blood nor what he seemed; and, for my part, I'm rayther o' that way o' thinkin' myself; for I never yet see'd

a common street Harab—as they calls them now—carry it
off like him. You might ha' heered a pin drop, as the
mate spoke.

"'Well, you young whelp,' says he, in his grimmest
voice, 'what's brought you here?'

"'It was my step-father as done it,' says the boy, in a
weak little voice, but as steady as could be. 'Father's
dead, and mother's married again, and my new father says
as how he won't have no brats about eatin' up his wages;
and he stowed me away when nobody warn't lookin', and
guv me some grub to keep me goin' for a day or two till I
got to sea. He says I'm to go to Aunt Jane, at Halifax;
and here's her address.' And with that, he slips his hand
into the breast of his shirt, and out with a scrap o' paper,
awful dirty and crumpled up, but with the address on it,
right enough.

"We all believed every word on't, even without the
paper; for his look, and his voice, and the way he spoke,
was enough to show that there warn't a ha'porth o' lyin'
in his whole skin. But the mate didn't seem to swallow
the yarn at all; he only shrugged his shoulders with a kind
o' grin, as much as to say, 'I'm too old a bird to be caught
by that kind o' chaff;' and then he says to him, 'Look
here, my lad, that's all very fine, but it won't do here—
some o' these men o' mine are in the secret, and I mean to
have it out of 'em. Now, you just point out the man as
stowed you away and fed you, this very minute; if you
doan't, it'll be the worse for you!'

"The boy looked up in his bright, fearless way (it did my
heart good to look at him, the brave little chap!) and says,
quietly, 'I've told you the truth; I ain't got no more to say.'

"The mate says nothin', but looks at him for a minute
as if he'd see clean through him; and then he faced round
to the men, lookin' blacker than ever. 'Reeve a rope to
the yard!' he sings out, loud enough to raise the dead;
'smart now!'

" The men all looked at each other, as much as to say: ' What on earth's a-comin' now ?' But aboard ship, o' course, when you're told to do a thing, you've got to do it ; so the rope was rove in a jiffy.

" ' Now, my lad,' says the mate, in a hard, square kind o' voice that made every word seem like fittin' a stone into a wall, ' you see that 'ere rope ? Well, I'll give you ten minutes to confess ; and if you don't tell the truth afore the time's up, I'll hang you like a dog !'

" The crew all stared at one another as if they couldn't believe their ears (I didn't believe mine, I can tell ye), and then a low growl went among 'em, like a wild beast awakin' out of a nap.

" ' Silence, there !' shouts the mate, in a voice like the roar of a nor'easter. ' Stand by to run for'ard !' as he held the noose ready to put it round the boy's neck. The little feller never flinched a bit; but there was some among the sailors (big strong chaps, as could ha' felled an ox) as shook like leaves in the wind. As for me, I bethought myself o' my little curly-haired lad at home, and how it 'ud be if any one was to go for to hang him ; and at the very thought on't I tingled all over, and my fingers clinched theirselves as if they was a-grippin' somebody's throat. I clutched hold o' a hand-spike, and held it behind my back, all ready.

" ' Tom,' whispers the chief-engineer to me, ' d'ye think he really means to do it ?'

" ' I don't know,' says I, through my teeth ; ' but if he does, he shall go first, if I swings for it !'

" I've been in many an ugly scrape in my time, but I never felt 'arf as bad as I did then. Every minute seemed as long as a dozen ; an' the tick o' the mate's watch, reg'-lar, pricked my ears like a pin. The men were very quiet, but there was a precious ugly look on some o' their faces ; and I noticed that three or four on 'em kep' edgin' for'ard to where the mate was, in a way that meant mischief. As

for me, I'd made up my mind that if he did go for to hang
the poor little chap, I'd kill him on the spot, and take my
chance.

" 'Eight minutes,' says the mate, his great deep voice
breakin' in upon the silence like the toll o' a funeral bell.
'If you've got anything to confess, my lad, you'd best out
with it, for ye're time's nearly up.'

" ' I've told you the truth,' answers the boy, very pale, but
as firm as ever. 'May I say my prayers, please ?'

" The mate nodded, and down goes the poor little chap
on his knees and puts up his poor little hands to pray. I
couldn't make out what he said (fact, my head was in sich
a whirl that I'd hardly ha' knowed my own name), but I'll
be bound God heard it, every word. Then he ups on his
feet again, and puts his hands behind him, and says to the
mate quite quietly, 'I'm ready !'

" And then, sir the mate's hard, grim face broke up all
to once, like I've seed the ice in the Baltic. He snatched
up the boy in his arms, and kissed him and burst out
a-cryin' like a child ; and I think there warn't one of us as
didn't do the same. I know I did for one.

" ' God bless you, my boy !' says he, smoothin' the child's
hair with his great hard hand. 'You're a true English-
man, every inch of you : you wouldn't tell a lie to save
your life ! Well, if so be as yer father's cast yer off, I'll
be yer father from this day forth ; and if I ever forget you,
then may God forget me !'

" And he kep' his word, too. When we got to Halifax
he found out the little un's aunt, and gev her a lump o'
money to make him comfortable ; and now he goes to see
the youngster every voyage, as reg'lar as can be ; and to
see the pair on 'em together—the little chap so fond of him,
and not bearin' him a bit o' grudge—it's 'bout as pretty
a sight as ever I seed. And now, sir, axin' yer parding,
it's time for me to be goin' below ; so I'll just wish yer
good-night."

"SURLY TIM'S TROUBLE."

MRS. FRANCES HODGSON BURNETT.

A LANCASHIRE STORY.

From Scribner's Monthly.

ABRIDGED FOR PUBLIC READING.

Surly Tim is represented to have been an operative in one of the large manufactories in the north of England. He had gained the name of "Surly Tim" through his strange demeanor toward his companions, often refusing to answer their questions or perform any of the ordinary civilities, on account of which his fellow workmen had given him the cold shoulder and dubbed him "Surly Tim." But one of the partners of the firm took a great deal of interest in Tim, thinking there must be something beneath the rough exterior, and so endeavored from time to time to draw him out, but without success, until one night, as he was going home, he chanced to pass the village churchyard, and heard a noise as of a man in distress just over the fence. Getting over to speak to him, he discovered that the man was none other than Surly Tim, sitting by two graves, one the longer and the other a shorter. Shortly, being grateful for the sympathy thus extended him, "Surly Tim" begins to tell his story, and why it is that he conducts himself as he does. It seems that some years before he had been married to a very lovely woman; but that she had previously been married to a soldier, one Phil Brent, who had beaten and abused her and finally deserted her and gone into the army, and whom she had heard by letter was killed at the Crimea. Supposing herself free again, of course, she had married Tim. He, after describing the courtship up to a little time before their marriage, says of her in his broad north-of-England dialect:

Rosanna Brent an' me got to be good friends, an' we walked home together o' nights, an' talked about our bits o' wage, an' our bits o' debt, an' th' way that wench 'ud keep me up i' spirits when I were a bit down-hearted about owt, wur just a wonder. An' bein' as th' lass wur so dear to me, I made up my mind to ax her to be summat dearer. So once goin' home wi' her, I takes hold o' her hand an'

lifts it up an' kisses it gentle—as gentle an' wi' summat th'
same feelin' as I'd kiss the Good Book.

" 'Sanna," I says, " bein' as yo've had so much trouble
wi' yo're first chance, would yo' be afeard to try a second ?
Could yo' trust a mon again ? Such a mon as me, 'Sanna ?"

" I wouldna be feart to trust thee, Tim," she answers
back soft an' gentle after a manner. " I wouldna be feart
to trust thee any time."

I kisses her hand again, gentler still.

" God bless thee, lass," I says. " Does that mean yes ?"

She crept up closer to me i' her sweet, quiet way.

" Aye, lad," she answers. " It means yes, an' I'll bide
by it."

" An' tha shalt never rue it, lass," said I. " Tha's gi'en
thy life to me, an' I'll gi' mine to thee, sure an' true."

So we wur axed i' th' church th' next Sunday, an' a
month fra' then we were wed ; an' if ever God's sun shone
on a happy mon, it shone on one that day, when we come
out o' church together—me an' Rosanna—an' went to our
bit o' a home to begin life again. I couldna tell thee, Mester—theer bean't no words to tell how happy an' peaceful
we lived fur two year after that. My lass never altered
her sweet ways, an' I just loved her to make up to her fur
what had gone by. I thanked God-a'-moighty fur his
blessin' every day, an' every day I prayed to be made worthy
of it. An' here's just wheer I'd like to ax a question,
Mester, about summat 'at's worretted me a good deal. I
dunnot want to question th' Maker, but I would loike to
know how it is 'at sometime it seems 'at we're clean forgot
—as if He couldna fash hissen about our troubles, an' most
loike left 'em to work out theirsens ? Yo' see, Mester, and
we aw see sometime, He thinks on us an' gi's us a lift; but
hasna tha thysen seen times when tha stopt short and axed
thysen, " Wheer's God-a'-moighty, 'at he disna straighten
things out a bit ? Th' world's i' a power o' a snarl. Th'
righteous is forsaken, 'n' his seed's beggin' bread. An' th'

devil's topmost again." I've talked to my lass about it
sometime, an' I dunnot think I meant harm, Mester, for I
felt humble enough—an' when I talked, my lass she'd listen an' smile soft and sorrowful, but she never gi' me but
one answer.

" 'Tim," she'd say, "this is on'y th' skoo', an' we're the
scholars, an' He's teachin' us His way. The Teacher wouldna be o' much use, Tim, if the scholars knew as much as he
did, an' I allers think it's th' best to comfort mysen wi'
sayin', ' The Lord-a'-moighty, he knows.'"

At th' eend o' th' year th' child wur born, th' little lad
here," touching the turf with his hand, " ' Wee Wattie '
his mother ca'd him, an' he wur a fine, lightsome little chap.
He filled th' whole house wi' music day in an' day out,
crowin' an' crowin'—an' cryin' too, sometime.

Well, Mester, before th' spring wur out Wee Wat was
toddlin' round, holdin' to his mother's gown, an' by th'
middle o' th' next he was cooin' like a dove, an' prattlin'
words i' a voice like hers. Happen we set too much store
by him, or happen it wur on'y th' Teacher again teachin'
us His way, but hows'ever that wur, I came home one
sunny mornin' fro' th' factory, an' my dear lass met me at
th' door all white an' cold, but tryin' hard to be brave an'
help me to bear what she had to tell.

" Tim," said she, " th' Lord ha' sent us trouble ; but we
can bear it together, canna we, dear lad ?"

That wur aw, but I knew what it meant, though th' poor
little lamb had been well enough when I kissed him last.

I went in an' saw him lyin' theer on his pillows, strug-
glin' an' gaspin' in hard convulsions, an' I seed aw was
over. An' in half an hour, just as the sun crept across th'
room an' touched his curls, th' pretty little chap opens his
eyes aw at once.

" Daddy !" he crows out. " Sithee Dad—" an' he lifts
hissen up, catches at th' floatin' sunshine, laughs at it, and
fa's back—dead, Mester.

I've allers thowt 'at th' Lord-a'-moighty knew what he wur doin' when he gi' th' woman t' Adam i' the Garden o' Eden. He knowed he wur nowt but a poor chap as couldna do for hissen; an' I suppose that's th' reason he gi' the woman th' strength to bear trouble when it comn. I'd ha' gi'n clean in if it hadna been fur my lass when th' little chap deed.

But the day comn when we could bear to talk about him, an' moind things he'd said an' tried to say i' his broken, babby way. An' so we were creepin' back again to th' old happy quiet, an' we had been for welly six month, when summat fresh comn. I'll never forget it, Mester, th' neet it happened. I'd kissed Rosanna at th' door, and left her standin' theer when I went up to th' village to buy summat she wanted. It wur a bright moonlight neet, just such a neet as this, an' the lass had followed me out to see th' moonshine, it wur so bright an' clear; an' just before I starts she folds both her hands on my shoulder an' says, soft and thoughtful:

"Tim, I wonder if the little chap sees us?"

"I'd loike to know, dear lass," I answers back. An' then she speaks again:

"Tim, I wonder if he'd know he was ours if he could see, or if he'd ha' forgot. He wur such a little fellow."

Them wur th' last peaceful words I ever heerd her speak. I went up to th' village an' getten what she sent me fur, an' then I comn back.

She wasna outside, an' I couldna see a leet about th' house, but I heerd voices, so I walked straight in—into th' entry an' into th' kitchen, an' theer she wur, Mester—my poor wench, crouching down by th' table, hidin' her face i' her hands, and close beside her wur a mon—a mon i' red sojer clothes.

My heart leaped into my throat, an' fur a minnit I hadna a word, fur I saw summat wur up, though I couldna tell what it wur. But at last my voice comn back.

" Good evenin', Mester," I says to him ; " I hope yo' ha'
not broughten ill news ? What ails thee, dear lass ?"

She stirs a little, and gives a moan like a dyin' child ; an'
then she lifts up her wan, broken-hearted face, an' stretches
out both her hands to me.

" Tim," she says, " dunnot hate me, lad, dunnot. I
thowt he wur dead long sin'. I thowt 'at th' Rooshans
killed him an' I wur free, but I amna. I never wur. He
never deed, Tim, an' theer he is—the mon as I wur wed to
an' left by. God forgi' him, an' oh, God forgi' me !"

Theer, Mester, theer's a story fur thee. My poor lass
wasna my wife at aw—th' little chap's mother wasna his
feyther's wife, an' never had been. That theer worthless
fellow as beat an' starved her an' left her to fight th' world
alone, had comn back alive an' well. He could tak' her
away fro' me any hour i' th' day, an' I couldna say a word
to bar him. Th' law said my wife—th' little dead lad's
mother—belonged to him, body an' soul. Theer was no
law to help us—it wur aw on his side.

" Tha canna want me now, Phil," she said. " Tha canna
care fur me. Tha must know I'm more this mon's wife
than thine. But I dunnot ax thee to gi' me to him, because
I know that wouldna be reet ; I on'y ax thee to let me
alone. I'll go fur enough off an' never see him more."

But the villain held to her. If she didna come wi' him,
he said, he'd ha' me up before th' court fur bigamy. I
could ha' done murder then, Mester, an' I would ha' done,
if it hadna been for the poor lass runnin' in betwixt us an'
pleadin' wi' aw her might. If we'n been rich foak theer
might ha' been some help fur her ; at least th' law might
ha' been browt to mak' him leave her be, but bein' poor
workin' foak theer was on'y one thing : th' wife mun go wi'
th' husband, an' theer th' husband stood—a scoundrel,
cursing, wi' his black heart on his tongue.

" Well," says th' lass at last, fair wearied out wi' grief,
"I'll go wi' thee, Phil, an' I'll do my best to please thee,

but I wunnot promise to forget th' mon as has been true
to me, an' has stood betwixt me an' th' world."

Then she turned round to me.

"Tim," she says, "surely he wunnot refuse to let us go
together to th' little lad's grave—fur th' last time." She
didna speak to him but to me, an' she spoke still an'
strained as if she wur too heart-broke to be wild. Her face
was as white as th' dead, but she didna cry, as any other
woman would ha' done. "Come, Tim," she said, "he
canna say no to that."

An' so out we went, an' we didna say a word until we
come to this very place, Mester.

We stood here for a minnit silent, an' then I sees her
begin to shake, an' she throws hersen down on th' grass wi'
her arms flung o'er th' grave, an' she cries out as ef her
death-wound had been give to her.

"Little lad," she says, "little lad, dost ta see thee
mother? Canst na tha hear her callin' thee? Little lad,
get nigh to th' Throne an' plead!"

I fell down beside o' th' poor crushed wench an' sobbed
wi' her. I couldna comfort her, fur wheer wur there any
comfort for us? Theer wur none left—theer wur no hope.
We was shamed an' broke down—our lives was lost. Th'
past wur nowt—th' future wur worse. Oh, my poor lass,
how hard she tried to pray—for me, Mester—yes, fur me,
as she lay theer wi' her arms round her dead babby's
grave, an' her cheek on th' grass as grew o'er his breast.
"Lord God-a'-moighty!" she says, "help us—dunnot gi'
us up—dunnot, dunnot! We canna do 'thowt thee now, if
th' time ever wur when we could. Th' little chap mun be
wi' Thee— I moind th' bit o' comfort about getherin' th'
lambs i' His bosom. An', Lord, if tha could spare him a
minnit, send him down to us wi' a bit o' lect. Oh, Feyther! help th' poor lad here—help him. Let th' weight
fa' on me, not on him. Just help th' poor lad to bear it.
If ever I did owt as wur worthy i' Thy sight, let that be

my reward. Dear Lord-a'-moighty, I'd be willin' to gi' up a bit o' my own heavenly glory fur th' dear lad's sake."

Well, Mester, she lay theer on th' grass prayin' and cry-in', wild but gentle, fur nigh haaf an hour, an' then it seemed 'at she got quiet loike, an' she got up. Happen th' Lord had hearkened an' sent th' child—happen He had —fur when she getten up her face looked to me aw white an' shinin' i' th' clear moonlight.

"Sit down by me, dear lad," she said, "an' hold my hand a minnit." I set down an' took hold of her hand, as she bid me.

"Tim," she said, "this wur why th' little chap deed. Dostna tha see now 'at th' Lord knew best ?"

"Yes, lass," I answers humble, an' lays my face on her hand, breakin' down again.

"Hush, dear lad," she whispers, "we hannot time fur that. I want to talk to thee. Wilta listen ?"

"Yes, wife," I says, an' I heerd her sob when I said it, but she catches hersen up again.

"I want thee to mak' me a promise," said she. "I want thee to promise never to forget what peace we ha' had. I want thee to remember it allers, an' to moind him 'at's dead, an' let his little hand howd thee back fro' sin an' hard thowts. I'll pray fur thee neet an' day, Tim, an' tha shalt pray fur me, an' happen theer'll come a leet. But ef theer dunnot, dear lad—an' I dunnot see how theer could—if theer dunnot, an' we never see each other agen, I want thee to mak' me a promise that if tha sees th' little chap first tha'lt moind him o' me, and watch out wi' him nigh th' gate, and I'll promise thee that if I see him first, I'll moind him o' thee an' watch out true an' constant."

I promised her, Mester, as yo' can guess, an' we kneeled down an' kissed th' grass, and she took a bit o' th' sod to put i' her bosom. An' then we stood up an' looked at each other, an' at last she put her dear face on my breast, an'

kissed me, as she had done every neet siu' we were mon
an' wife.

"Good-bye, dear lad," she whispers—her voice aw
broken. " Doan't come back to th' house till I'm gone;
good-bye, dear, dear lad, an' God bless thee !" An' she
slipped out o' my arms an' wur gone in a moment, awmost
before I could cry out.   *   *   *

The whole of this beautiful story, with others from Mrs. Burnett's
charming pen, may be found in a book of hers, called " Surly Tim
and other Stories," published by Scribner, Armstrong & Co., N. Y.

THE WATER-MILL.

D. C. McCallum.

Oh ! listen to the water-mill, through all the live-long day,
As the clicking of the wheels wears hour by hour away;
How languidly the autumn wind doth stir the withered leaves,
As on the field the reapers sing, while binding up the sheaves !
A solemn proverb strikes my mind, and as a spell is cast,
"The mill will never grind again with water that is past."

The summer winds revive no more leaves strewn o'er earth and
      main,
The sickle never more will reap the yellow garnered grain;
The rippling stream flows ever on, aye tranquil, deep and still,
But never glideth back again to busy water-mill.
The solemn proverb speaks to all, with meaning deep and vast,
"The mill will never grind again with water that is past."

Oh! clasp the proverb to thy soul, dear loving heart and true,
For golden years are fleeting by, and youth is passing too;
Ah ! learn to make the most of life, nor lose one happy day,
For time will ne'er return sweet joys neglected, thrown away;
Nor leave one tender word unsaid, thy kindness sow broadcast—
"The mill will never grind again with water that is past."

Oh! the wasted hours of life that have swiftly drifted by,
Alas! the good we might have done, all gone without a sigh;
Love that we might once have saved by a single kindly word,

Thoughts conceived but ne'er expressed, perishing, unpenned,
    unheard.
Oh! take the lesson to thy soul, forever clasp it fast,
"The mill will never grind again with water that is past."

Work on while yet the sun doth shine, thou man of strength and
    will,
The streamlet ne'er doth useless glide by clicking water-mill;
Nor wait until to-morrow's light beams brightly on thy way,
For all that thou canst call thine own lies in the phrase "to-day:"
Possessions, power, and blooming health must all be lost at last—
"The mill will never grind again with water that is past."

Oh! love thy God and fellow man, thyself consider last,
For come it will when thou must scan dark errors of the past;
Soon will this fight of life be o'er, and earth recede from view,
And heaven in all its glory shine where all is pure and true.
Ah! then thou'lt see more clearly still the proverb deep and vast,
"The mill will never grind again with water that is past."

THE FALL OF THE PEMBERTON MILL.
ELIZABETH STUART PHELPS.
Abridged for Public Reading.

The following is a vivid description of the terrible disaster which
took place at Lawrence, Mass., January 10th, 1860. It is taken
from "The Tenth of January," a story of love, jealousy and heroism, ending in the awful sacrifice here portrayed. The entire story
can be found in a work by the same author, entitled, "MEN,
WOMEN AND GHOSTS," published by James R. Osgood & Co.

[The writer describes Lawrence as "unique in its way," and says,
"Of the twenty-five thousand souls who inhabit that city, ten
thousand are operatives in the factories. Of these ten thousand,
two-thirds are girls."

Asenath Martyn was slightly built and undersized. The children used to cry out, "Humpback! Humpback!" and people in
passing would say, "Look at that girl!" Her face was gravely
lined, but womanly and pleasant. The author says, "She puzzled
one at the first glance, and at the second. An artist, meeting her

musing on a canal-bridge one day, went home and painted a May-
flower budding in February." The world had, indeed, dealt harsh-
ly with her. Her deformity had been caused by a blow at the
hands of a drunken mother. Sene remembered that, and her un-
happy childhood; and when the wretched mother had met a vio-
lent death, she also remembered having heard some one say at the
funeral, "How glad Sene must be!" Since that, life had meant
three things—her father, the mills, and Richard Cross. The latter
had, by chance, become a resident of the same home with Sene
and her old father. A tender sympathy, combined with a one-
ness of interests, soon ripened into love and resulted in an engagement.

After a time Sene discovered that Dick's affections were being
drawn away from herself and centred upon Del Ivory, a pretty,
fascinating, giddy creature, whose beauty she sometimes envied,
but whose frivolity she despised. Dick, not knowing his secret
was discovered, was too honorable to think of breaking his engagement, and consequently attempted to resist and suppress his new
love by avoiding Del and redoubling his attentions to Sene. The
latter had long been trying to release him, but could not find the
courage to do so; and he, seeing that she suffered, wearied himself with plans to make her eyes shine; and did she try to speak
her wretched secret, he suffocated her with kindness, and struck
her dumb with tender words. It was the morning after the last
of these ineffectual attempts on Sene's part that this reading opens.]

The silent city steeped and bathed itself in rose-tints;
the river ran red, and the snow crimsoned on the distant
New Hampshire hills; Pemberton, mute and cold, frowned
across the disk of the climbing sun, and dripped, as she
had seen it drip before, with blood.

The day broke softly, the snow melted, the wind blew
warm from the river. The factory-bell chimed cheerily,
and a few sleepers, in safe, luxurious beds, were wakened
by hearing the girls sing on their way to work.

*   *   *   *   *

Sene was a little dizzy that morning—the constant pal-
pitation of the floors always made her dizzy after a wake-

ful night—and so her colored cotton threads danced out of place and troubled her.

Dell Ivory, working beside her, said, " How the mill shakes ! What's going on ?"

" It's the new machinery they're h'isting in," observed the overseer, carelessly. " Great improvement, but heavy, very heavy ; they calc'late on getting it all into place to-· day ; you'd better be tending to your frame, Miss Ivory."

 *   *   *   *   *

Years before, an unknown workman in South Boston, casting an iron pillar upon its core, had suffered it to " float " a little, a very little more, till the thin, unequal side cooled to the measure of an eighth of an inch. That man had provided Asenath's way of escape.

She went out at noon with her luncheon, and found a place upon the stairs, away from the rest, and sat there awhile, with her eyes upon the river, thinking. She could not help wondering a little, after all, why God need to have made her so unlike the rest of his fair handiwork. Del came bounding by, and nodded at her carelessly. Two young Irish girls, sisters—the beauties of the mill—magnificently colored creatures—were singing a little love-song together, while they tied on their hats to go home.

" There *are* such pretty things in the world !" thought poor Sene.

Did anybody speak to her after the girls were gone ? Into her heart these words fell suddenly, " *He* hath no form nor comeliness. *His* visage was so marred more than any man."

They clung to her fancy all the afternoon. She liked the sound of them. She wove them in with her black and dun colored threads.

The wind began at last to blow chilly up the staircases, and in at the cracks ; the melted drifts out under the wall to harden ; the sun dipped above the dam ; the mill dimmed slowly ; shadows crept down between the frames.

" It's time for lights," said Meg Match, and swore a little at her spools.

Sene, in the pauses of her thinking, heard snatches of the
girls' talk.

" Going to ask out to-morrow, Meg ?"

" Guess so, yes; me and Bob Smith we thought we'd go
to Boston, and come up in the theatre train."

" Del Ivory, I want the pattern of your zouave."

" Did I go to church ? No, you don't catch me ! If I
slave all the week, I'll do what I please on Sunday."

" Hush-sh ! There's the boss looking over here !"

" Kathleen Donnavon, be still with your ghost stories.
There's one thing in the world I never will hear about, and
that's dead people."

" Del," said Sene, " I think to-morrow—"

She stopped. Something strange had happened to her
frame; it jarred, buzzed, snapped : the threads untwisted
and flew out of place.

" Curious !" she said, and looked up.

Looked up to see her overseer turn wildly, clap his hands
to his head, and fall ; to hear a shriek from Del that froze
her blood ; to see the solid ceiling gape above her ; to see
the walls and windows stagger ; to see iron pillars reel, and
vast machinery throw up its helpless, giant arms, and
a tangle of human faces blanch and writhe !

She sprang as the floor sunk. As pillar after pillar
gave way, she bounded up an inclined plane, with the
gulf yawning after her. It gained upon her, leaped at her,
caught her ; beyond were the stairs and an open door ;
she threw out her arms, and struggled on with hands and
knees, tripped in the gearing, and saw, as she fell, a
square, oaken beam above her yield and crash ; it was of a
fresh red color ; she dimly wondered why—as she felt her
hands slip, her knees slide, support, time, place and reason
go utterly out.

" *At ten minutes before five, on Tuesday, the tenth of Jan-*

uary, the Pemberton Mill, all hands being at the time on duty, fell to the ground."

So the record flashed over the telegraph wires, sprang into large type in the newspapers, passed from lip to lip, a nine days' wonder, gave place to the successful candidate and the muttering South, and was forgotten.

Who shall say what it was to the seven hundred and fifty souls who were buried in the ruins ? What to the eighty-eight who died that death of exquisite agony ? What to the wrecks of men and women who endure unto this day a life that is worse than death ? What to that architect and engineer who, when the fatal pillars were first delivered to them for inspection, had found one broken under their eyes, yet accepted the contract, and built with them a mill whose thin walls, and wide, unsupported stretches might have tottered over massive columns and on flawless ore ?

Sene's father, working at Meg Match's shoes—she was never to wear those shoes, poor Meg!—heard, at ten minutes before five, what he thought to be the rumble of an earthquake under his very feet, and stood with bated breath, waiting for the crash. As nothing further appeared to happen, he took his stick and limped out into the street.

A vast crowd surged through it from end to end. Women with white lips were counting the mills—Pacific, Atlantic, Washington—Pemberton ! Where was Pemberton ?

Where Pemberton had winked its many eyes last night, and hummed with its iron lips this noon, a cloud of dust, black, silent, horrible, puffed a hundred feet into the air.

Asenath opened her eyes after a time. Beautiful green and purple lights had been dancing about her, but she had had no thoughts. It occurred to her now that she must have been struck upon the head. The church-clocks were striking eight. A bonfire which had been built at a distance, to light the citizens in the work of rescue, cast a little gleam in through the *debris* across her two hands, which lay clasped together at her side. One of her fingers, she saw, was gone; it was the finger which held Dick's little engagement ring. The red beam lay across her forehead, and drops dripped from it upon her eyes. Her feet, still tangled in the gearing which had tripped her, were buried beneath a pile of bricks.

A broad piece of flooring, that had fallen slantwise, roofed her in, and saved her from the mass of ironwork overhead, which would have crushed the breath out of Hercules. Fragments of looms, shafts and pillars were in heaps about. Some one whom she could not see was dying just behind her. A little girl who worked in her room—a mere child—was crying, between her groans, for her mother. Del Ivory sat in a little open space, cushioned about with reels of cotton; she had a shallow gash upon her cheek; she was wringing her hands. They were at work from the outside, sawing entrances through the labyrinth of planks. A dead woman lay close by, and Sene saw them draw her out. It was Meg Match. One of the pretty Irish girls was crushed quite out of sight; only one hand was free; she moved it feebly. They could hear her calling for Jimmy Mahoney, Jimmy Mahoney! and would they be sure and give him back the handkerchief? Poor Jimmy Mahoney! By-and-by she called no more; and in a little while the hand was still. On the other side of the slanted flooring some one prayed aloud. She had a little baby at home. She was asking God to take care of it for her. " For Christ's sake," she said. Sene listened for the Amen, but it was never spoken. Beyond they dug a man out from under a dead body, unhurt. He crawled to his feet, and broke into furious blasphemies.

Del cried presently that they were cutting them out. The glare of bonfires struck through an opening; saws and axes flashed; voices grew distinct.

" They never can get at me," said Sene. "I must be

able to crawl. If you could get some of those bricks off of my feet, Del !"

Del took off two or three in a frightened way ; then seeing the blood on them, sat down and cried.

A Scotch girl, with one arm shattered, crept up and removed the pile, then fainted.

The opening broadened, brightened; the sweet night-wind blew in; the safe night-sky shone through. Sene's heart leaped within her. Out in the wind and under the sky she should stand again, after all ! Back in the little bright kitchen, where the sun shone, and she could sing a song, there would yet be a place for her. She thought of her father, of Dick, of the supper-table set for three. Life —even her life, grew sweet, now that it was slipping from her. She worked her head from under the beam, and raised herself upon her elbow. At that moment she heard a cry :

" Fire ! *fire !* GOD ALMIGHTY HELP THEM—THE RUINS ARE ON FIRE !"

A man working over the *debris* from the outside had taken the notion—it being rather dark just there—to carry a lantern with him.

" For God's sake," a voice cried from the crowd, " don't stay there with that light !"

But before the word had died upon the air, it was the dreadful fate of the man with the lantern to let it fall, and it broke upon the ruined mass.

That was at nine o'clock. What there was to see from then till morning could never be told or forgotten.

A network twenty feet high, of rods and girders, of beams, pillars, stairways, gearing, roofing, ceiling, walling ; wrecks of looms, shafts, twisters, pulleys, bobbins, mules, locked and interwoven ; wrecks of human creatures wedged in ; a face that you know turned up at you from some pit which twenty-four hours' hewing could not open; a voice that you know crying after you from God knows where ; a mass of long, fair hair visible here, a foot there, three fingers of a hand over there; the snow bright-red underfoot; charred limbs and headless trunks tossed about; strong men carrying covered things by you, at sight of which other strong men have fainted; the little yellow jet that flared up, and died in smoke, and flared again, leaped out, licked the cotton bales, tasted the oiled machinery, crunched the netted wood, danced on the heaped-up stone, threw its cruel arms high into the night, roared for joy at helpless firemen, and swallowed wreck, death and life together out of your sight—the lurid thing stands alone in the gallery of tragedy.

"Del," said Sene, presently, "I smell the smoke." And in a little while, "How red it is growing away over there at the left!"

To lie here and watch the hideous redness crawling after her, springing at her!—it had seemed greater than reason could bear, at first.

Now it did not trouble her. She grew a little faint, and her thoughts wandered. She put her head down upon her arm, and shut her eyes. Dreamily she heard them saying a dreadful thing outside, about one of the overseers; at the alarm of fire he had cut his throat, and before the flames touched him he was taken out. Dreamily she heard Del cry that the shaft behind the heap of reels was growing hot. Dreamily she saw a tiny puff of smoke struggle through the cracks of a broken fly-frame.

They were working to save her, with rigid, stern faces. A plank snapped, a rod yielded; they drew out the Scotch girl; her hair was singed; then a man with blood upon his face and wrists held down his arms.

"There's time for one more! God save the rest of ye—I can't!"

Del sprang; then stopped—even Del—stopped ashamed, and looked back at the cripple.

Asenath at this sat up erect. The latent heroism in her awoke. All her thoughts grew clear and bright. The tangled skein of her perplexed and troubled winter unwound suddenly. This, then, was the way. It was better so. God had provided himself a lamb for the burnt offering.

So she said, " Go, Del, and tell him I sent you with my dear love, and that it's all right."

And Del at the first word went.

Sene sat and watched them draw her out; it was a slow process; the loose sleeve of her factory sack was scorched.

Somebody at work outside turned suddenly and caught her. It was Dick. The love which he had fought so long broke free of barrier in that hour. He kissed her pink arm where the burnt sleeve fell off. He uttered a cry at the blood upon her face. She turned faint with the sense of safety ; and, with a face as white as her own, he bore her away in his arms to the hospital, over the crimson snow.

Asenath looked out through the glare and smoke with parched lips. For a scratch upon the girl's smooth cheek, he had quite forgotten her. They had left her, tombed alive here in this furnace, and gone their happy way. Yet it gave her a curious sense of relief and triumph. If this were all that she could be to him, the thing which she had done was right, quite right. God must have known. She turned away, and shut her eyes again.

When she opened them, neither Dick, nor Del, nor crimsoned snow, nor sky, were there; only the smoke writhing up a pillar of blood-red flame.

The child who had called for her mother began to sob out that she was afraid to die alone.

"Come here, Molly," said Sene. " Can you crawl around ?"

Molly crawled around.

" Put your head in my lap, and your arms about my waist, and I will put my hands in yours—so. There! I guess that's better."

But they had not given them up yet. In the still unburnt rubbish at the right, some one had wrenched an opening within a foot of Sene's face. They clawed at the solid iron pintles like savage things. A fireman fainted in the glow.

"Give it up!" cried the crowd from behind. "It can't be done! Fall back!"—then hushed, awe-struck.

An old man was crawling along upon his hands and knees over the heated bricks. He was a very old man. His gray hair blew about in the wind.

"I want my little gal!" he said. "Can't anybody tell me where to find my little gal?"

A rough-looking young fellow pointed in perfect silence through the smoke.

"I'll have her out yet. I'm an old man, but I can help. She's my little gal, ye see. Hand me that there dipper of water; it'll keep her from choking, may be. Now! keep cheery, Sene! Your old father 'll get ye out. Keep up good heart, child! That's it!"

"It's no use, father. Don't feel bad, father. I don't mind it very much."

He hacked at the timber; he tried to laugh; he bewildered himself with cheerful words.

"No more ye needn't, Senath, for it'll be over in a minute. Don't be downcast yet! We'll have ye safe at home before ye know it. Drink a little more water—do now! They'll get at ye now, sure!"

But above the crackle and roar a woman's voice rang out like a bell:

"We're going home, to die no more."

A child's notes quavered in the chorus. From sealed and unseen graves, white young lips swelled the glad refrain—

"We're going, going home."

The crawling smoke turned yellow, turned red. Voice after voice broke and hushed utterly. One only sang on like silver. It flung defiance down at death. It chimed into the lurid sky without a tremor. For One stood beside her in the furnace, and His form was like unto the form of the Son of God. Their eyes met. Why should not Ascnath sing?

"Senath!" cried the old man out upon the burning bricks; he was scorched now, from his gray hair to his patched boots.

The answer came triumphantly:

"To die no more, no more, no more!"

"Sene! little Sene!"

But some one pulled him back.

DEATH OF LITTLE JO.
From "Bleak House."

Jo is very glad to see his old friend; and says, when they are left alone, that he takes it uncommon kind as Mr. Sangsby should come so far out of his way on accounts of sich as him. Mr. Sangsby, touched by the spectacle before him, immediately lays upon the table half-a-crown, that magic balsam of his for all kinds of wounds.

"And how do you find yourself, my poor lad?" inquires the stationer, with his cough of sympathy.

"I'm in luck, Mr. Sangsby, I am," returns Jo, "and don't want for nothink. I'm more cumf'bler nor you can't think, Mr. Sangsby. I'm wery sorry that I done it, but I didn't go fur to do it, sir."

The stationer softly lays down another half-crown, and asks him what it is that he is sorry for having done.

"Mr. Sangsby," says Jo, "I went and giv a illness to the lady as wos and yet as warn't the t'other lady, and none of 'em never says nothink to me for having done it, on accounts of their being so good and my having been s' unfortnet. The lady come herself and see me yes'day, and she ses, 'Ah Jo!' she ses. 'We thought we'd lost

you, Jo !' she ses. And she sits down a smilin' so quiet,
and don't pass a word nor yit a look upon me for having
done it, she don't, and I turns agin the wall, I doos, Mr.
Sangsby. And Mr. Jarnders, I see him a forced to turn
away his own self. And Mr. Woodcot, he come fur to
give me somethink fur to ease me, wot he's allus a doin'
on day and night, and w'en he come a-bendin' over me
and a-speakin' up so bold, I see his tears a-fallin', Mr.
Sangsby."

The softened stationer deposits another half-crown on
the table. Nothing less than a repetition of that infallible
remedy will relieve his feelings.

" Wot I wos thinkin' on, Mr. Sangsby," proceeds Jo,
" wos, as you wos able to write wery large, p'raps ?"

" Yes, Jo, please God," returns the stationer.

" Uncommon precious large, p'raps ?" says Jo, with
eagerness.

" Yes, my poor boy."

Jo laughs with pleasure. " Wot I wos thinkin' on then,
Mr. Sangsby, wos, that wen I wos moved on as fur as ever
I could go, and couldn't be moved no furder, whether you
might be so good, p'raps, as to write out, wery large, so
that any one could see it anywheres, as that I wos wery
truly hearty sorry that I done it, and that I never went fur
to do it ; and that though I didn't know nothink at all, I
know'd as Mr. Woodcot once cried over it, and wos allus
grieved over it, and that I hoped as he'd be able to forgive
me in his mind. If the writin' could be made to say it
wery large he might."

" It shall say it, Jo ; very large."

Jo laughs again. " Thankee, Mr. Sangsby. It's wery
kind of you, sir, and it makes me more comfbler nor I wos
afore."

The meek little stationer, with a broken and unfinished
cough, slips down his fourth half-crown—he has never been
so close to a case requiring so many—and is fain to depart.

And Jo and he, upon this little earth, shall meet no more.
No more.

(*Another Scene.—Enter Mr. Woodcot.*)

" Well, Jo, what is the matter ?   Don't be frightened."

" I thought," says Jo, who has started, and is looking
round, "I thought I was in Tom-all-Alone's agin.   An't
there nobody here but you, Mr. Woodcot ?"

" Nobody."

" And I an't took back to Tom-all-Alone's, am I, sir ?"

" No."

Jo closes his eyes, muttering, " I am wery thankful."

After watching him closely a little while, Allan puts his
mouth very near his ear, and says to him in a low, distinct
voice :   " Jo, did you ever know a prayer ?"

" Never know'd nothink, sir."

" Not so much as one short prayer ?"

"No, sir.   Nothink at all.   Mr. Chadbands he wos a
prayin' wunst at Mr. Sangsby's and I heerd him, but he
sounded as if he wos a-speakin' to hisself, and not to me.
He prayed a lot, but *I* couldn't make out nothink on it.
Different times there wos other gen'l'men come down Tom-
all-Alone's a-prayin', but they all mostly sed as the t'other
wuns prayed wrong, and all mostly sounded to be a-talkin'
to theirselves, or a-passing blame on the t'others, and not
a-talkin' to us.   *We* never know'd nothink.   *I* never
know'd what it wos all about."

It takes him a long time to say this ; and few but an ex-
perienced and attentive listener could hear, or, hearing,
understand him.   After a short relapse into sleep or
stupor, he makes, of a sudden, a strong effort to get out of
bed.

"Stay, Jo, stay !   What now ?"

" It's time for me to go to that there berryin' ground,
sir," he returns with a wild look.

" Lie down, and tell me.   What burying ground, Jo ?"

" Where they laid him as wos wery good to me ; wery

good to me, indeed, he wos. It's time for me to go down
to that there berryin' ground, sir, and ask to be put along
with him. I wants to go there and be berried. He used
for to say to me, ' I am as poor as you, to-day, Jo,' he ses.
I wants to tell him that I am as poor as him, now, and
have come there to be laid along with him."

"By-and-by, Jo ; by-and-by."

" Ah ! P'rhaps they wouldn't do it if I wos to go myself.
But will you promise to have me took there, sir, and laid
along with him ?"

" I will, indeed."

" Thankee, sir ! Thankee, sir ! They'll have to get the
key of the gate afore they can take me in, for it's allus
locked. And there's a step there, as I used fur to clean
with my broom—it's turned wery dark, sir. Is there any
light a-comin' ?"

" It is coming fast, Jo."

Fast. The cart is shaken all to pieces, and the rugged
road is very near its end.

" Jo, my poor fellow !"

" I hear you, sir, in the dark, but I'm a-gropin'—a-gropin'
let me catch hold of your hand."

" Jo, can you say what I say ?"

" I'll say anything as you say, sir, for I knows it's good."

"OUR FATHER."

" Our Father !—yes, that's wery good, sir."

" WHICH ART IN HEAVEN."

" Art in Heaven !—Is the light a-comin', sir ?"

" It is close at hand. HALLOWED BE THY NAME."

" Hallowed be—thy—name !"

The light is come upon the dark benighted way. Dead.
Dead, your Majesty. Dead, my lords and gentlemen.
Dead, Right Reverends and Wrong Reverends of every
order. Dead, men and women, born with heavenly com-
passion in your hearts. And dying thus around us every
day !

THE SOLDIER'S REPRIEVE.
Abridged for Public Reading.

" I thought, Mr. Allan, when I gave my Bennie to his country, that not a father in all this broad land made so precious a gift—no, not one. The dear boy only slept a minute, just one little minute, at his post; I know that was all, for Bennie never dozed over a duty. How prompt and reliable he was! I know he only fell asleep one little second—he was so young, and not strong, that boy of mine! Why, he was as tall as I, and only eighteen! and now they shoot him because he was found asleep when doing sentinel duty. Twenty-four hours, the telegram said—only twenty-four hours. Where is Bennie now ?"

" We will hope, with his heavenly Father," said Mr. Allan, soothingly.

" Yes, yes; let us hope; God is very merciful!

" ' I should be ashamed, father,' Bennie said, ' when I am a man, to think I never used this great right arm'— and he held it out so proudly before me—' for my country, when it needed it. Palsy it rather than keep it at the plow.'

" ' Go, then, go, my boy,' I said, ' and God keep you !' God has kept him, I think, Mr. Allan !" and the farmer repeated these last words slowly, as if, in spite of his reason, his heart doubted them.

" Like the apple of his eye, Mr. Owen; doubt it not."

Blossom sat near them listening, with blanched cheek. She had not shed a tear. Her anxiety had been so concealed that no one had noticed it. She had occupied herself mechanically in the household cares. Now she answered a gentle tap at the kitchen door, opening it to receive from a neighbor's hand a letter. " It is from him," was all she said.

It was like a message from the dead ! Mr. Owen took

the letter, but could not break the envelope, on account of his trembling fingers, and held it toward Mr. Allan, with the helplessness of a child.

The minister opened it, and read as follows:

"DEAR FATHER:—When this reaches you I shall be in eternity. At first, it seemed awful to me; but I have thought about it so much now, that it has no terror. They say they will not bind me, nor blind me; but that I may meet my death like a man. I thought, father, it might have been on the battle-field, for my country, and that, when I fell, it would be fighting gloriously; but to be shot down like a dog for nearly betraying it—to die for neglect of duty! O father, I wonder the very thought does not kill me! But I shall not disgrace you. I am going to write you all about it; and when I am gone, you may tell my comrades. I cannot now.

"You know I promised Jemmie Carr's mother I would look after her boy; and when he fell sick I did all I could for him. He was not strong when he was ordered back into the ranks, and the day before that night, I carried all his luggage, beside my own, on our march. Towards night we went in on double-quick, and though the luggage began to feel very heavy, everybody else was tired too; and as for Jemmie, if I had not lent him an arm now and then, he would have dropped by the way. I was all tired out when we came into camp, and then it was Jemmie's turn to be sentry, and I *would* take his place; but I was too tired, father. I could not have kept awake if a gun had been pointed at my head; but I did not know it until—well, until it was too late."

"God be thanked!" interrupted Mr. Owen, reverently. "I knew Bennie was not the boy to sleep *carelessly* at his post."

"They tell me to-day that I have a short reprieve, given to me by circumstances—'time to write to you,' our good colonel says. Forgive him, father, he only does his duty;

he would gladly save me if he could; and do not lay my death up against Jemmie. The poor boy is broken-hearted, and does nothing but beg and entreat them to let him die in my stead.

"I can't bear to think of mother and Blossom. Comfort them, father! Tell them I die as a brave boy should, and that, when the war is over, they will not be ashamed of me, as they must be now. God help me; it is very hard to bear! Good-by, father! God seems near and dear to me; not at all as if He wished me to perish forever, but as if He felt sorry for His poor, sinful, broken-hearted child, and would take me to be with Him and my Saviour in a better, better life."

A deep sigh burst from Mr. Owen's heart. "Amen," he said solemnly, "Amen."

"To-night, in the early twilight, I shall see the cows all coming home from pasture, and precious little Blossom stand on the back stoop, waiting for me! But I shall never, never come! God bless you all! Forgive your poor Bennie."

Late that night the door of the "back stoop" opened softly, and a little figure glided out, and down the footpath that led to the road by the mill. She seemed rather flying than walking, turning her head neither to the right nor to the left, looking only now and then to Heaven, and folding her hands as if in prayer. Two hours later, the same young girl stood at the Mill Depot, watching the coming of the night train; and the conductor, as he reached down to lift her into the car, wondered at the tear-stained face that was upturned toward the dim lantern he held in his hand. A few questions and ready answers told him all; and no father could have cared more tenderly for his only child, than he for our little Blossom. She was on her way to Washington, to ask President Lincoln for her brother's life. She had stolen away, leaving only a note to tell where and why she had gone. She had brought

Bennie's letter with her; no good, kind heart, like the President's, could refuse to be melted by it. The next morning they reached New York, and the conductor hurried her on to Washington. Every minute, now, might be the means of saving her brother's life. And so, in an incredibly short time, Blossom reached the Capital, and hastened immediately to the White House.

The President had but just seated himself to his morning task, of overlooking and signing important papers, when, without one word of announcement, the door softly opened, and Blossom, with downcast eyes and folded hands, stood before him.

" Well, my child," he said, in his pleasant, cheerful tones, " what do you want, so bright and early in the morning ?"

" Bennie's life, please, sir," faltered Blossom.

" Bennie ? Who is Bennie ?"

" My brother, sir. They are going to shoot him for sleeping at his post."

" Oh, yes ;" and Mr. Lincoln ran his eye over the papers before him. " I remember. It was a fatal sleep. You see, child, it was at a time of special danger. Thousands of lives might have been lost for his culpable negligence."

" So my father said," replied Blossom, gravely, " but poor Bennie was so tired, sir, and Jemmie so weak: He did the work of two, sir, and it was Jemmie's night, not his ; but Jemmie was too tired, and Bennie never thought about himself, that he was tired, too."

" What is this you say, child ? Come here ; I do not understand," and the kind man caught eagerly, as ever, at what seemed to be a justification of an offense.

Blossom went to him; he put his hand tenderly on her shoulder, and turned up the pale, anxious face towards his. How tall he seemed ! and he was President of the United States, too. A dim thought of this kind passed for a moment through Blossom's mind; but she told her simple and straightforward story, and handed Mr. Lincoln Bennie's letter to read.

He read it carefully; then, taking up his pen, wrote a few hasty lines, and rang his bell.

Blossom heard this order given : " *Send this dispatch at once.*"

The President then turned to the girl and said, "Go home, my child, and tell that father of yours, who could approve his country's sentence, even when it took the life of a child like that, that Abraham Lincoln thinks the life far too precious to be lost. Go back, or—wait until to-morrow ; Bennie will need a change after he has so brave-ly faced death ; he shall go with you."

" God bless you, sir," said Blossom; and who shall doubt that God heard and registered the request ?

Two days after this interview, the young soldier came to the White House with his little sister. He was called into the President's private room, and a strap fastened upon the shoulder. Mr. Lincoln then said: " The soldier that could carry a sick comrade's baggage, and die for the act so uncomplainingly, deserves well of his country." Then Bennie and Blossom took their way to their Green Moun-tain home. A crowd gathered at the Mill Depot to wel-come them back ; and, as farmer Owen's hand grasped that of his boy, tears flowed down his cheeks, and he was heard to say fervently : " *The Lord be praised !*"

BROTHER ANDERSON.

THOMAS K. BEECHER

I was to preach for brother Anderson. He was a good pastor. Almost the last time I saw him he had just called upon a lamb of his flock to ask after her spiritual welfare, and for fifty cents toward his salary. He had left his tub and brushes at the foot of the hill, and he re-

sumed them when he had made his call; for, like the
great apostlo, he used to labor, working with his own
hands.

Punctual to the hour, brother Anderson came rolling
across the street, and up to the door, and we went in together. After the usual songs and prayers, I took for my
text Paul's counsel to the Corinthians as to their disorder-
ly meetings and meaningless noises. The sermon was,
in the main, a reading of the fourteenth chapter of Paul's
first letter, with comments and applications interspersed.
I spoke for half an hour, and while showing consideration
for the noisy ways of my audience, exhorted them to cul-
tivate intelligence as well as passion.

"When you feel the glory of God in you, let it out, of
course. Shout Glory, clap your hands, and all that. But
stop now and then, and let some wise elder stand up and
tell what it all means. Men and boys hang round your
windows, and laugh at you and religion, because they don't
understand. Some men have religion all in their heads;
others in their hearts. Now you must have it in your heads
and hearts."

As I sat down Brother Anderson stood on the pulpit
step to give out a hymn.

I am not certain that he could read, for he stood book in
hand, and seemingly from memory gave the number
of the hymn, and repeated the first two stanzas with deep
and growing feeling. Of the third he read three lines :

> One army ob de livin' God
>   To his comman' we bow ;
> Part of hos (t) 'ov cross'er flood,
>   An' part——

Here he stopped, and after swallowing one or two
chokes, went on to say : I love Brudder Beecher. I love
to hear him preach. He's told us a good many things.
He's our good fr'en. An' he sez dat some folks goes up to
glory noisy 'n shoutin', and some goes still-like, 'z if they's

'shamed of wat's in 'em. And he sez we'd better be more like de still-kind, an' de white-kind, an' de white folk will like us more. But den I tinks 'taint much 'count no way, wedder we goes up still-like or shoutin', cause heaven's a mighty big place, brudder; an' wen we all goes marchin' up to see de Lord, an' I's so full ob de lub, and de joy, and de glory, dat I mus' clap my han's an' shout, de good Lord's got some place war we won't 'sturb nobody, and we can shout, Glory! Glory! Bress de Lord! I'm safe, I'm safe in glory at las'; I tell you, brudders an' sisters, dat heaven's a mighty big place, and dere's room dare for brudder Beecher an' us too.

" Brudder Beecher says de engines on de railroad only puff, puff, regular breathin'-like, when dey's at work haulin de big loads, and dat de bell and whistle don't do no work, dey only make a noise; guess dat's so. I don't know 'bout ingins much, and I don't know wedder I's a puff-puff ingin, or wedder I blow de whistle an' rings de bell. I feels like bofe (with a chuckle) sometimes! An' I tell you what, wen de fire is a burnin', an' I gets de steam up, don't dribe no cattle on de track!

" An' de boys an' gals, an' de clarks an' young lawyers, dey come up yar watch-nights, and dey peep in de winders, an' stan' roun' de doors, an' dey laugh an' make fun of 'lig'n! An' Brudder Beecher sez, why don't we stop de noise now'n den, an' go out an' tell 'em 'bout it—'splain it to 'em? An' I 'members what de Bible says 'bout de outer darkness, an' de weepin', an' de wailin', an' de gnashin' ob de teef. An' if dese boys an' gals stan' dar outside a-laffin', bimeby dey'll come to de wailin' an' de weepin' fus' dey know. An' den when dey stan' roun' de great temple ob de Lord, an' see de glory shinin' out, an' de harpers harpin', and all de music, an' de elders bowin', an' all de shoutin' like many waters, an' all de saints a-singin' ' Glory to de Lam'!' s'pose God'll say, 'Stop dat ar noise dar, Gabr'l; you Gabr'l go out an' 'splain'?

" Yes, I see dem stan' las' winter 'roun' de doors an' under de winders an' laff; an' dey peek in an' laff. An' I
'member wot I saw last summer 'mong de bees. Some ob
de hives was nice, an' clean an' still, like 'spectable meetin's,
an' de odders was a bustin' wid honey ; an' de bees kep'
a-goin' an' a-comin' in de clover ; an' dey jes kep' on a-fill-
in' up de hive, till de honey was a-flowin' like de lan' of
Canaan. An' I saw all 'roun' de hives was de ants an'
worms, an' de great drones, an' black bugs, an' dey kep'
on de outside. Dey wasn' bees. Dey couldn' make de
honey for darselves. Dey couldn' fly to de clover an' de
honey-suckle. Dey jes' hung 'roun' de bustin' hive, an'
lived on de drippin's.

" An' de boys an' gals come up yar, an' hang 'roun'.
Jes' come in, an' we'll show you how de gospel bees do.
Come in an' we'll lead you to de clover ! Come in—we'll
make your wings grow. Come in ! won't ye ? Well den,
poor things, let 'em stan' 'roun' de outside, an' hab de
drippin's. We's got honey in dis hive.

> Part of 'e hos' av cross 'er flood,
> An' part are crossin' now.

" Sing, brudders, sing." And they sang. * * *

A BASKET OF FLOWERS.

SARAH BRIDGES STEBBINS.

Abridged for Public Reading.

A few days afterward the Light of the Household went
forth into the poor places of the neighborhood and brought
in, one by one, shrinking children, with shabby garments
and shy glances; little girls ungathered into schools, untaught of ignorant parents who were slaves of labor, to
whom was preached no Gospel of salvation from idleness,
weakness or vice. These, allured in unwillingly at first,
hard enough for a time to keep together, came at last into

this quiet chamber as to a holy shrine, sat earnestly at the feet of a pale, patient teacher, and learned the ways of truth and right. Day by day—for a few minutes only sometimes, sometimes for hours, according to her fluctuating strength—she had them with her, and in the poor homes where they belonged the mothers listened with a sort of awe to the accounts of this pale lady, lying always on her couch, covered with the white, fleecy folds of her delicate work, and giving out to little rapt listeners thoughts that would abide with them all their lives.

After a while Christmas was drawing near, and one day there was an interesting assemblage of these small scholars in a room where one of them lived, whose mother was a washerwoman, and upon tubs and buckets they were seated in a circle ; and the subject of their meeting and consultation was, How to Get a Christmas Present for the Crippled Sister, and what It Should Be.

Strange and various articles were proposed, to which many objections were raised, principally by the little President, who seemed to think her most important duty was to keep the intended expenditure within the limits of the probable amount, for which purpose she was obliged to do a good many sums out loud. The puzzle was growing deeper, and the likelihood of a decision seemed farther off than ever, when Nettie Blane said, in her soft voice : " I know what the lady loves more than anything else, and that's flowers ! Why, just here a while ago, before it got so cold, I found a bunch of wild posies growing alongside the road as I was going to her house ; they were just common things, but I picked them and took them to her, and you just ought to have seen her over them ! Her face lit all up, she was so pleased, and do you know that for a minute she looked like she never was sick at all; and she kind of petted them with her fingers, and thanked me so nice that I never was so glad of doing anything in my life !"

" But flowers die so soon, and then she would never

have nothin' to keep to make her feel that we'd bin thinkin' of her!"

An anxious shade fell over Nettie Blane's face, that, however, instantly brightened with a new thought.

"Oh, yes, she would," she said, "because she'd always remember! Don't you know, somehow, if you once get a thing, you've always got it, even if you don't see it? If I sell my shells, it don't much matter, really, because whenever I think about them, they'll always be in my heart, and I'll always know that Uncle Jim he brought them to me over the sea!"

Some one murmured, "Things ought to be awful pretty to be remembered always!" and the general consent seemed to settle without dispute that a basket of flowers would be the very sweetest thing in the world to give.

"And I know of a man who keeps a hot-house just out of town," said the young President, "and he looks good-humored and kind, so maybe he'll give us something real nice for what we'll have to pay!" And soon after the meeting dispersed.

The day before Christmas, as the big, burly and rosy owner of the conservatory just out of town was sorting his choicest blooms for a large wedding which was to take place in the evening, the door of the hot-house suddenly opened, and a squadron of a dozen or more small girls entered in solemn procession.

"Bless my soul!" said the Gentle Giant, turning his bluff, bright face toward them, "what do you young ones want?"

For an instant they had stood quite still, looking about them in wonder and delight; for the whole place was so filled with rare and lovely blossoms that its atmosphere, color, and profusion was like a concentration of the tropics.

"If you please, sir, we want to buy a basket of flowers."

The man dropped the two or three buds he held in his hand, turned entirely around, and gave one steady look down the whole line; he saw at once that they were not likely to want flowers for themselves, and imagined that one or two had been sent on a message, and that the rest had accompanied these.

" *You*—want—to—*buy* "—he said slowly.

" Yes, sir, a basket of flowers, if you please."

" Who for ? and why are there so many of you ?"

" Well, sir, I'll tell you. You see, sir, there's a dear kind lady, and she is a cripple, and never gets off a low kind of bed she lays on, and works all the time the most beautiful 'broidering flowers you ever seen. And she teaches us; so we thought we'd like to give her a Christmas present, and we've all saved up till we think we've got enough ; and because she never can go out to see anything a-growing, and just loves flowers like they were alive, we made up our minds to take her some ; because we all give something toward it we all came together about it ; and if you please, sir, we'd like as nice a basketful as you can make up for our money."

The rosy face bloomed out bright as one of his own blossoms; the round eyes grew wonderfully soft and moist, as the big burly man stooped and kissed the small speaker, and said, with just a touch of huskiness in his voice :

" Well, you're a blessed little party ! You just go round, all of you, and pick out what you'd like to have, and I'll fix them up for you !" There was an immediate stir in the young procession, and evident delight in this permission, and an intention to put it instantly into practice, when the Small Leader called out, " You keep still there, will you ? I've got something else to say!"

Curiosity restored order, and she again addressed the gardener.

" Ain't those grand flowers very dear ? You see, sir, we don't want anything we can't pay for all right. We've got this much money ; please to count it, sir, and see if it will do !" And she handed him a rather battered tin match-box containing the accumulated contributions in small coins, as they had been gradually brought in as they were gained.

The Big Gardener by this time was too much touched to keep quite calm. "Here," he said to the Little Leader, " you count out this money, and tell me how much it is, and I'll do the best I can for it !" And when he took a basket and went round his hot-house collecting here and there his simplest blooms, all these keen eyes watched him in unbroken silence, and not one of them stirred a gaze from his fingers as he laid in the moss, propped a superb, stainless lily in the centre, and arranged round it with exquisite taste violets and heart's-ease, and delicate, pure blossoms; in breathless quiet they noted every flower that was woven into its place, little thinking that these commoner plants which they were used to see in summer were almost as costly as foreign growths in winter; and it was not till the whole was finished that they broke out into exclamations of satisfaction.

" This must be a mighty good woman to make you love her so !" said the man as he handed over the basket to the careful hold of the Little Leader.

" Good!" answered Nettie Blane, "she's a-most an angel ; it seems like she ought never to do anything but stand up close to the Throne with just such lilies in her hand !"

For Nettie's inmost heart was stirred by the flowers and the occasion.

The Big Gardener looked at her a second as if he thought she might have been a stray cherub herself.

" That's all your own gift," he said, pointing to the lily-crowned basket ; " but would you mind taking her a little present from me too ?"

" It shall only be one flower," he said ; and as a single flower in their inexperienced eyes could not possibly compare with a basketful, a happy assent was immediately given.

He went round among his plants to where bloomed one magnificent blossom, the only one of its kind in the green-house. He broke it from the stalk, and placed it in Nettie Blane's hand. " Oh, thank you !" said Nettie's glad voice, " I will give it to her with your compliments." And then the Big Gardener kissed every one of them as they passed out, and stood at his hot-house door, and watched the little procession as it wound out of sight with the Little Leader at the head, carrying the Basket of Flowers.

*   *   *   *   *   *

MAHSR JOHN.

IRWIN RUSSELL.

From Scribner's Monthly.

I heahs a heap o' people talkin', ebrywhar I goes,
'Bout Washintnm an' Franklum, an' sech genuses as dose :
I s'pose dey's mighty fine, but heah's de p'int I's bettin' on—
Dere wuzn't nar a one ob 'em come up to Mahsr John.

He shorely wuz de grates' man de country ebber growed—
You better had git out de way when *he* come 'long de road!
He hel' his head up dis way, lik' he 'spised to see de groun';
An' niggers had to toe de mark when Mahsr John wuz 'roun'.

I only has to shet my eyes, an' den it seems to me
I sees him right afore me now, jes' like he use' to be,
A-settin' on de gal'ry lookin' awful big an' wise,
Wid little niggers fannin' him to keep away de flies.

He alluz wore de berry bes' ob planters' linen suits,
An' kep' a nigger busy jus' a-blackin' ob his boots;
De buckles on his galluses wuz made of solid gol',
An' diamon's !—dey wuz in his shu't as thick as it would hol'.

You heered me ! 'twas a caution, when he went to take a ride,
To see him in de kerridge, wid ol' Mistis by his side—

Mulatter Bill a-dribin', an' a nigger on behin';
An' two Kaintucky hosses tuk 'em tearin' whar dey gwine.

Ol' Mahsr John wuz pow'ful rich—he owned a heap o' lan';
Fibe cotton places, 'sides a sugar place in Loozyan';
He had a thousan' nigger—an' he worked 'em shore's you born!
De oberseahs ud start 'em at de breakin' ob de morn.

Sometimes he'd gib a frolic—dat's de time you seed de fun;
De 'ristocratic fam'lies, dey ud be dar, ebry one,
Dey'd hab a band from New Orleans to play for 'em to dance,
An' tell you what, de *supper* wuz a *'tickler* sarcumstance.

Well, times is changed! De war it come an' sot de niggers free,
An' now ol' Mahsr John ain't hardly wuf as much as me;
He had to pay his debts, an' so his lan' is mos'ly gone—
An' I declar' I's sorry for pore ol' Mahsr John.

But when I heah 'em talkin' 'bout some sullybrated man,
I listens to 'em quiet, till dey done said all dey can,
An' den I 'lows dot in dem days, 'at I remembers on,
Dat gemman warn't a patchin' onto my ol' Mahsr John!

DADDY FLICK'S SPREE.

D. L. PROUDFIT.

Daddy Flick was a queer old Dick,
Trudging along with a crooked stick,
Frowsy and dirty and tattered and torn,
Wearing a hat that a goat would scorn
To nibble at, it was so forlorn;
And I state, with a solemn regard for truth,
That a garment must be in a state of ruth,
A very unsavory species of game,
If an up-town goat will reject the same.
He was gray as a badger and old as a crow,
And his eyes were queer—well, beery, you know,
Bleached and weak—and he had, I suppose,
The most absurd and peculiar nose

That ever invited a passer-by
To think of the worth of sobriety.
Naught can I say in his praise, I wot.
Respectable? Honest? Oh, certainly not!
Most people called him a wretched old sot.
Only a beggar. He used to stand,
Day by day, with his hat in his hand,
Asking for pence from the grave and the gay,
And getting them, too, I am glad to say,
Not in abundance, but just enough
For a little bread, and more of the stuff
That went to nourish his curious nose
And keep it blooming, a full-blown rose.
" Life," he said, " for the rich or poor,
Means but the same—endure, endure !
Troubles to poor and rich befall,
But the bottle," he said, "is a friend to all."

Now that you know the old reprobate,
Beggar, dishonest, inebriate,
All that he asks, sir, of you or me
Is a little measure of charity.

For twenty years he had been the same,
Till at last the usual period came
When age began to assert itself,
And threatened to lay him upon the shelf,
And parties said in that part of the town,
That the poor old sinner was breaking down,
When all at once he seemed to be
Displaying a greater activity—
Begging with more than his usual vim,
And, what was entirely new for him,
Picking up jobs, and inquiring, too,
For any work he could find to do.
People said it was strange, if true,
When they heard a rumor to that effect—
A change impossible to expect.
It seemed, you perceive, anomalous
That Flick should be turning industrious.

But so it was; if you'll listen well,
The bottom facts of the case I'll tell.

    *   *   *   *   *   *

Flick, for seventy years to date,
Had never thought to be bothering fate;
Had been contented to barely live,
Caring for nothing the world can give—
A sort of philosopher, as I think,
In seeking for naught but his meat and drink;
But, mind you, never a notion had he
Of any claim to philosophy.

The greatest and wisest have one soft streak,
And so at the last Flick showed up weak.
He said to himself on a certain day,
"Daddy Flick, you are old and gray,
Likely to drop off any day.
Before your coffin is lowered down,
Or, what is worse, you go on the town,
You ought to have, as it seems to me,
One good old-fashioned, expensive spree."

Alas, I fear that my readers all
Are disappointed at such a fall.
I wish he had felt a higher call,
Something of nobler and healthier tone—
An aspiration with more backbone.
But I told you before that the poor old rat
Had never a virtue beneath his hat.
(I must tell my stories as they befall;
If you don't like 'em don't read 'em, that's all.)

After a couple of months had passed
Daddy Flick had at length amassed
A sum sufficient, he thought, to see
His way to that same old-fashioned spree.
And so, one night as he paddled home,
He said to himself that the time had come
And, cackling over an ancient song,
He jingled his cash as he went along.

What were his assets? A marvelous sum;
Enough to purchase unlimited rum—
(Listen, you who collect your rents!)
About a dollar and fifty cents.

Passing along by a vacant lot
(The name of the street I have clean forgot),
A very diminutive boy he spied,
Slouching a very tall fence beside:
A lonesome figure, so woe-begone,
So desolate-looking and haggard and wan,
That even Flick in his callous heart
Felt a movement of pity start.
Ragged he was, and exceedingly small,
With garments that covered him, that was all;
A cap remarkable after its kind,
With front dismantled and baggy behind;
Shoes too big by about a mile,
But gaping wide with a frightful smile,
As though they laughed at the tiny feet
That dragged such a burden along the street.
He stood there listless and weary and worn,
Hands in his pockets, alone and forlorn;
His features stained with the dirty streaks
Of the tears that had dried on his little cheeks.

Flick was none of your tender sort;
Philanthropy never had been his forte;
But the look of the child was so woefully sad
That he stopped and spoke to the little lad,
And got the story I'll tell to you,
Since it only requires a line or two:
His mother had died in a drunken fit,
He was hungry, and that was the whole of it.

Flick, as you know, was all primed for a spree;
All the same he said, " Come with me!"
And took the child to his narrow den,
And fed him and kept him that night, and then,
To cut it short, he put up the tin

He had labored so long and so hard to win,
And started the boy in the paper trade,
Where he prospered well, and a living made.

Then Flick returned to his ancient ways,
And loafed and begged through the listless days;
Cracking, by way of amusing folk,
An occasional rummy and senile joke;
But what is the funniest thing to me,
He always thought he had had that spree,
And bragged about it to every one
That for once in his life he had had some fun.

  * * * * * *

THE BALLAD OF BABIE BELL.

T. B. ALDRICH.

Have you not heard the poets tell
How came the dainty Babie Bell
  Into this world of ours?
The gates of heaven were left ajar;
With folded hands and dreamy eyes,
Wandering out of Paradise,
She saw this planet, like a star,
  Hung in the glistening depths of even—
Its bridges running to and fro,
O'er which the white-winged angels go,
  Bearing the holy dead to heaven.
She touched a bridge of flowers—those feet,
So light they did not bend the bells
Of the celestial asphodels!
They fell like dew upon the flowers,
Then all the air grew strangely sweet—
And thus came dainty Babie Bell
  Into this world of ours.
She came and brought delicious May.
  The swallows built beneath the eaves;
  Like sunlight in and out the leaves,

The robins went the livelong day;
The lily swung its noiseless bell,
   And o'er the porch the trembling vine
   Seemed bursting with its veins of wine.
How sweetly, softly, twilight fell!
Oh, earth was full of singing-birds,
And opening spring-tide flowers,
When the dainty Babie Bell
   Came to this world of ours!

O Babie, dainty Babie Bell,
How fair she grew from day to day!
What woman-nature filled her eyes,
What poetry within them lay!
Those deep and tender twilight eyes,
   So full of meaning, pure and bright,
   As if she yet stood in the light
Of those ope'd gates of Paradise.
And so we loved her more and more;
Ah, never in our hearts before
   Was love so lovely born:
We felt we had a link between
This real world and that unseen—
   The land beyond the morn.
And for the love of those dear eyes,
For love of her whom God led forth
(The mother's being ceased on earth
When Babie came from Paradise)—
For love of Him who smote our lives,
   And woke the chords of joy and pain,
We said, *Dear Christ!*—our hearts bent down
   Like violets after rain.

And now the orchards, which were white
And red with blossoms when she came,
Were rich in autumn's mellow prime.
The clustered apples burnt like flame,
The soft-cheeked peaches blushed and fell,
The ivory chestnut burst its shell,
The grapes hung purpling in the grange;

And time wrought just as rich a change
    In little Babie Bell.
Her lissome form more perfect grew,
    And in her features we could trace,
    In softened curves, her mother's face !
Her angel-nature ripened too.
We thought her lovely when she came,
But she was holy, saintly now—
Around her pale, angelic brow ·
We saw a slender ring of flame.

God's hand had taken away the seal
    That held the portals of her speech ;
And oft she said a few strange words
    Whose meaning lay beyond our reach.
She never was a child to us,
We never held her being's key,
We could not teach her holy things ;
    She was Christ's self in purity.

It came upon us by degrees ;
We saw its shadow ere it fell,
The knowledge that our God had sent
His messenger for Babie Bell.
We shuddered with unlanguaged pain,
And all our hopes were changed to fears,
And all our thoughts ran into tears
    Like sunshine into rain.
We cried aloud in our belief,
"Oh, smite us gently, gently, God !
Teach us to bend and kiss the rod,
And perfect grow through grief."
Ah, how we loved her, God can tell ;
Her heart was folded deep in ours,
    Our hearts are broken, Babie Bell !

At last he came, the messenger,
    The messenger from unseen lands :
And what did dainty Babie Bell ?
She only crossed her little hands,
She only looked more meek and fair !

We parted back her silken hair,
We wove the roses round her brow—
White buds, the summer's drifted snow—
Wrapt her from head to foot in flowers;
And then went dainty Babie Bell
    Out of this world of ours!

AUX ITALIENS.

OWEN MEREDITH.

AT THE ITALIAN OPERA.

At Paris it was, at the Opera there;
    And she looked like a queen in a book, that night,
With the wreath of pearl in her raven hair,
    And the brooch on her breast, so bright.

Of all the operas that Verdi wrote,
    The best, to my taste, is the Trovatore;
And Mario can soothe with a tenor note
    The souls in purgatory.

The moon on the tower slept soft as snow;
    And who was not thrilled in the strangest way,
As we heard him sing, while the gas burned low,
    " *Non ti scordar di me!*"

The Emperor there, in his box of state,
    Looked grave, as if he had just then seen
The red flag wave from the city-gate,
    Where his eagles in bronze had been.

The Empress, too, had a tear in her eye.
    You'd have said that her fancy had gone back again,
For one moment, under the old blue sky,
    To the old glad life in Spain.

Well! there in our front-row box we sat
    Together, my bride-betrothed and I;
My gaze was fixed on my opera-hat,
    And hers on the stage hard by.

And both were silent, and both were sad.
    Like a queen, she leaned on her full white arm,
With that regal, indolent air she had ;
    So confident of her charm!

I have not a doubt she was thinking then
    Of her former lord, good soul that he was !
Who died the richest and roundest of men,
    The Marquis of Carabas.

I hope that, to get to the kingdom of heaven,
    Through a needle's eye he had not to pass ;
I wish him well for the jointure given
    To my lady of Carabas.

Meanwhile I was thinking of my first love,
    As I had not been thinking of aught for years,
Till over my eyes there began to move
    Something that felt like tears.

I thought of the dress that she wore last time,
    When we stood, 'neath the cypress-trees, together,
In that lost land, in that soft clime,
    In the crimson evening weather ;

Of that muslin dress (for the eve was hot),
    And her warm white neck in its golden chain.
And her full, soft hair, just tied in a knot,
    And falling loose again;

And the jasmin-flower in her fair young breast;
    Oh, the faint, sweet smell of that jasmin-flower,
And the one bird singing alone to his nest,
    And the one star over the tower.

I thought of our little quarrels and strife,
    And the letter that brought me back my ring,
And it all seemed then, in the waste of life,
    Such a very little thing!

For I thought of her grave below the hill,
    Which the sentinel cypress-tree stands over.
And I thought . . . . "were she only living still,
    How I could forgive her and love her!"

And I swear, as I thought of her thus, in that hour,
    And of how, after all, old things were best,
That I smelt the smell of that jasmin-flower,
    Which she used to wear in her breast.

It smelt so faint, and it smelt so sweet,
    It made me creep, and it made me cold!
Like the scent that steals from the crumbling sheet
    When a mummy is half unrolled.

And I turned and looked. She was sitting there
    In a dim box, over the stage; and drest
In that muslin dress, with that full soft hair,
    And that jasmin in her breast!

I was here, and she was there,
    And the glittering horseshoe curved between—
From my bride-betrothed, with her raven hair,
    And her sumptuous, scornful mien.

To my early love, with her eyes downcast,
    And over her primrose face the shade
(In short, from the Future back to the Past),
    There was but one step to be made.

To my early love from my future bride
    One moment I looked. Then I stole to the door,
I traversed the passage; and down at her side
    I was sitting, a moment more.

My thinking of her, or the music's strain,
    Or something which never will be exprest,
Had brought her back from the grave again,
    With the jasmin in her breast.

She is not dead, and she is not wed!
    But she loves me now, and she loved me then!
And the very first word that her sweet lips said,
    My heart grew youthful again.

The Marchioness there, of Carabas,
    She is wealthy, and young, and handsome still,
And but for her . . . . well, we'll let that pass—
    She may marry whomever she will.

But I will marry my own first love,
  With her primrose face ; for old things are best,
And the flower in her bosom, I prize it above
  The brooch in my lady's breast.

The world is filled with folly and sin,
  And Love must cling where it can, I say ;
For Beauty is easy enough to win,
  But one isn't loved every day.

And I think, in the lives of most women and men,
  There's a moment when all would go smooth and even,
If only the dead could find out when
  To come back and be forgiven.

But oh, the smell of that jasmin-flower !
  And oh, that music ! and oh, the way
That voice rang out from the donjon tower,
      Non ti scordar di me,
      Non ti scordar di me !

BREITMANN IN MARYLAND.

Der Breitmann mit his gompany
  Rode out in Marylandt.
" Dere's nichts to trink in dis countrie ;
  Mine troat's as dry as sand.
It's light canteen und haversack,
  It's hoonger mixed mit doorst ;
Und if we had some lager-bier
  I'd trink oontil I boorst.
      Gling, glang, gloria !
      We'd trink oontil we boorst.

" Herr Leut'nant, take a dozen men,
  Und ride dis land around !
Herr Feldwebel, go foragin'
  Dill somedings goot is found.
Gotts-doonder ! men, go ploonder !
  We hafn't trinked a bit

Dis fourdeen hours! If I had bier
  I'd sauf oontil I shplit!
    Gling, glarg, gloria!
We'd sauf oontil we shplit!"

At mitternacht a horse's hoofs
  Coom rattlin' troo de camp;
"Rouse dere!—coom rouse der house dere!
  Herr Copitain—we moost tromp!
De scouds have found a repel town,
  Mit repel davern near,
A repel keller in de cround,
  Mit repel lager bier!
    Gling, glang, gloria!
  All fool of lager bier!

Gottsdonnerkreuzschockschwerenoth!
  How Breitmann broked de bush!
"O let me see dat lager bier!
  O let me at him rush!
Und is mein sabre sharp und true,
  Und is mein war-horse goot?
To get one quart of lager bier
  I'd shpill a sea of ploot.
    Gling, glang, gloria!
  I'd shpill a sea of ploot.

"Fuenf hoonderd repels hold de down,
  One hunderd strong are we;
Who gares a tam for all de odds
  When men so dirsty pe?"
And in dey smashed and down dey crashed,
  Like donder-polts dey fly,
Rush fort as der wild yæger cooms
  Mit blitzen troo de shky.
    Gling, glang, gloria!
  Like blitzen troo de shky.

How flewed to rite, how flewed to left
  De moundains, drees unt hedge;
How left und rite de yæger corps
  Went donderin troo de pridge.

Und splash und splosh dey ford de shtream
  Where not some pridges pe :
All dripplin' in de moondlight peam
  Stracks went de cavallrie !
      Gling, glang, gloria !
    Der Breitmann's cavallrie !

Und hoory, hoory on dey rote,
  Oonheedin' vet or try ;
Und horse und rider shnort und blowed,
  Und shparklin' bepples fly.
Ropp ! ropp ! I shmell de barley-prew !
  Dere's somedings goot ish near.
Ropp ! Ropp !—I scent de kneiperei ;
  We've got to lager bier !
      Gling, glang, gloria !
    We've got to lager bier !

Hei ! how de carpine pullets klinged
  Oopon de helmets hart !
Oh, Breitmann—how dy sabre ringed ;
  Du alter Knasterbart !
De contrapands dey sing for choy
  To see de rebs go down,
Und hear der Breitmann grimly gry :
  Hoorah !—we've dook de down.
      Gling, glang, gloria !
    Victoria, victoria !
  De Dootch have dook de down.

Mid shout and crash and sabre flash,
  And wild husaren shout,
De Dootchmen boorst de keller in,
  Und rolled de lager out ;
And in the coorlin powder shmoke,
  While shtill de pullets sung,
Dere shtood der Breitmann, axe in hand,
  A-knockin' out de boong.
      Gling, glang, gloria !
    Victoria ! Encoria !
  De shpicket beats de boong.

Gotts! vot a shpree der Breitmann had
.   While yet his hand was red,
A-trinkin' lager from his poots
Among de repel tead.
'Twas dus dey went at mitternight
Along der moundain side ;
'Twas dus dey help make history !
Dis was der Breitmann's ride.
Gling, glang, gloria ;
Victoria ! Victoria !
Cer'visia, encoria ?
De treadful mitnight ride
Of Breitmann's wild Freischarlinger,
All famous, broad, und wide.

" THE MORNING ARGUS " OBITUARY DEPART-
MENT.   MAX ADELER.

A rather unusual sensation has been excited in the village by *The Morning Argus* within a day or two ; and
while most of the readers of that wonderful sheet have
thus been supplied with amusement, the soul of the editor
has been filled with gloom and wrath and despair. Colonel
Bangs recently determined to engage an assistant to take
the place made vacant by the retirement of the eminent
art-critic, Mr. Murphy, and he found in one of the lower
counties of the State a person who appeared to him to be
suitable. The name of the new man is Slimmer.

When Mr. Slimmer arrived, and entered upon the performance of his duties, Colonel Bangs explained his theory
to the poet, and suggested that whenever a death-notice
reached the office, he should immediately write a rhyme or
two which should express the sentiments most suitable to
the occasion.

Mr. Slimmer had charge of the editorial department the
next day, during the absence of Colonel Bangs in Wilming-
ton. Throughout the afternoon and evening death-notices

arrived; and when one would reach Mr. Slimmer's desk, he would lock the door, place the fingers of his left hand among his hair, and agonize until he succeeded in completing a verse that seemed to him to accord with his instructions.

The next morning Mr. Slimmer proceeded calmly to the office for the purpose of embalming in sympathetic verse the memories of other departed ones. As he came near to the establishment he observed a crowd of people in front of it, struggling to get into the door. Ascending some steps upon the other side of the street, he overlooked the crowd, and could see within the office the clerks selling papers as fast as they could handle them, while the mob pushed and yelled in frantic efforts to obtain copies, the presses in the cellar meanwhile clanging furiously. Standing upon the curbstone in front of the office, there was a long row of men, each of whom was engaged in reading *The Morning Argus*, with an earnestness that Mr. Slimmer had never before seen displayed by the patrons of that sheet. The bard concluded that either his poetry had touched a sympathetic chord in the popular heart, or that an appalling disaster had occurred in some quarter of the globe.

He went round to the back of the office and ascended to the editorial rooms. As he approached the sanctum, loud voices were heard within. Mr. Slimmer determined to ascertain the cause before entering. He obtained a chair, and placing it by the side door, he mounted it and peeped over the door through the transom. There sat Colonel Bangs, holding *The Morning Argus* in both hands, while the fringe which grew in a semi-circle around the edge of his bald head stood straight out, until he seemed to resemble a gigantic gun-swab. Two or three persons stood in front of him in threatening attitudes. Slimmer heard one of them say:

"My name is McGlue, sir! William McGlue! I am a

brother of the late Alexander McGlue. I picked up your
paper this morning, and perceived in it an outrageous insult
to my deceased relative, and I have come around to demand,
sir, WHAT YOU MEAN by the following infamous language:

> " 'The death-angel smote Alexander McGlue,
> And gave him protracted repose;
> He wore a checked shirt and a number nine shoe,
> And he had a pink wart on his nose.
> No doubt he is happier dwelling in space,
> Over there on the evergreen shore.
> His friends are informed that his funeral takes place
> Precisely at quarter past four.'

"This is simply diabolical! My late brother had no
wart on his nose, sir. He had upon his nose neither a
pink wart nor a green wart, nor a cream-colored wart, nor
a wart of any other color. It is a slander! It is a gratu-
itous insult to my family, and I distinctly want you to say
what do you mean by such conduct?"

"Really, sir," said Bangs, "it is a mistake. This is the
horrible work of a miscreant in whom I reposed perfect
confidence. He shall be punished by my own hand for
this outrage. A pink wart! Awful! sir—awful! The
miserable scoundrel shall suffer for this—he shall, indeed!"

"How could I know," murmured Mr. Slimmer, to the
foreman, who with him was listening, "that the corpse
hadn't a pink wart? I used to know a man named
McGlue, and *he* had one, and I thought *all* the McGlues
had. This comes of irregularities in families."

"And who," said another man, addressing the editor,
authorized you to print this hideous stuff about my deceased son? Do you mean to say, Bangs, that it is not
with your authority that your low comedian inserted with
my advertisement the following scandalous burlesque?
Listen to this:

> " 'Willie had a purple monkey climbing on a yellow stick,
> And when he sucked the paint all off it made him deathly sick;

And in his latest hours he clasped that monkey in his hand,
And bade good-bye to earth and went into a better land.

"'Oh, no more he'll shoot his sister with his little wooden gun;
And no more he'll twist the pussy's tail and make her yowl, for fun.
The pussy's tail now stands out straight; the gun is laid aside;
The monkey doesn't jump around since little Willie died.'

" The atrocious character of this libel will appear when
I say that my son was twenty years old, and that he died
of liver complaint."

" Infamous! utterly infamous!" groaned the editor, as
he cast his eyes over the lines. "And the wretch who
did this still remains unpunished! It is too much!"

" And yet," whispered Slimmer to the foreman, "he
told me to lighten the gloom and to cheer the afflicted
family with the resources of my art; and I certainly
thought that idea about the monkey would have that effect,
somehow.   Bangs is ungrateful!"

Just then there was a knock at the door, and a woman
entered, crying.

" Are you the editor?" she inquired of Colonel Bangs.
Bangs said he was.

" W-w-well!" she said in a voice broken by sobs,
" wh-what d'you mean by publishing this kind of poetry
about my child? M-my name is Sm-Smith; and wh-when
I looked this m-morning for the notice of Johnny's d-death
in your paper, I saw this scandalous verse:

"'Four doctors tackled Johnny Smith—
    They blistered and they bled him;
 With squills and anti-bilious pills
    And ipecac they fed him.
 They stirred him up with calomel,
    And tried to move his liver;
 But all in vain—his little soul
    Was wafted o'er the River.'

" It's false! false! and mean! Johnny only had *one*

doctor. And they d-didn't bl-bleed and bl-blister him. It's a wicked falsehood, and you're a hard-hearted brute f-f-for printing it !"

" Madam, I shall go crazy !" exclaimed Bangs. " This is not my work. It is the work of a villain whom I will slay with my own hand as soon as he comes in. Madam, the miserable outcast shall die !"

" Strange ! strange !" said Slimmer. " And this man told me to combine elevated sentiment with practical information. If the information concerning the squills and ipecac is not practical, I have misunderstood the use of that word. And if young Smith didn't have four doctors, it was an outrage. He ought to have had them, and they ought to have excited his liver. Thus it is that human life is sacrificed to carelessness."

While the poet mused, hurried steps were heard upon the stairs, and in a moment a middle-aged man dashed in abruptly, and seizing the colonel's scattered hair, bumped his prostrate head against the table three or four times with considerable force. Having expended the violence of his emotion in this manner, he held the editor's head down with one hand, shaking it occasionally by way of emphasis, and with the other hand seized the paper and said :

" You disgraceful old reprobate ! You disgusting vampire ! You hoary-headed old ghoul ! What d'you mean by putting such stuff as this in your paper about my deceased son ? What d'you mean by printing such awful doggerel as this, you depraved and dissolute ink-slinger—you imbecile quill-driver, you !

" 'Oh ! bury Bartholomew out in the woods,
   In a beautiful hole in the ground,
 Where the bumble-bees buzz and the woodpeckers sing,
   And the straddle-bugs tumble around ;
 So that, in winter, when the snow and the slush
   Have covered his last little bed,

His brother Artemus can go out with Jane
And visit the place with his sled.'

" I'll teach you to talk about straddle-bugs! I'll instruct
you about slush! I'll enlighten your insane old intellect
on the subject of singing woodpeckers! What do *you* know
about Jane and Artemus, you wretched buccaneer, you
despicable butcher of the English language? Go out with
a sled! I'll carry you out in a hearse before I'm done
with you, you deplorable lunatic !"

At the end of every phrase the visitor gave the editor's
head a fresh knock against the table. When the exercise
was ended, Colonel Bangs explained and apologized in the
humblest manner, promising at the same time to give his
assailant a chance to flog Mr. Slimmer, who was expected
to arrive in a few moments.

" The treachery of this man," murmured the poet to the
foreman, "is dreadful. Didn't he desire me to throw a
glamour of poesy over commonplace details? But for that
I should never have thought of alluding to woodpeckers
and bugs, and other children of nature. The man objects
to the remarks about the sled. Can the idiot know that it
was necessary to have a rhyme for 'bed'? Can he suppose that I could write poetry without rhymes? The man
is a lunatic ! He ought not to be at large !"

The poet determined to leave before any more criticisms
were made upon his performances. He jumped down from
his chair and crept softly toward the back staircase.

The story told by the foreman relates that Colonel Bangs
at the same instant resolved to escape any further persecu-
tion, and he moved off in the direction taken by the poet.
The two met upon the landing, and the colonel was about
to begin his quarrel with Slimmer, when an enraged old
woman who had been groping her way up-stairs suddenly
plunged her umbrella at Bangs, and held him in the corner while she handed a copy of the *Argus* to Slimmer, and
pointing to a certain stanza, asked him to read it aloud.

He did so in a somewhat tremulous voice, and with
frightened glances at the enraged colonel. The verse was
as follows :

> " Little Alexander's dead ;
>   Jam him in a coffin ;
>   Don't have as good a chance
>   For a fun'ral often ;
>   Rush his body right around
>   To the cemetery ;
>   Drop him in the sepulchre
>   With his Uncle Jerry."

The colonel's assailant accompanied the recitation with
such energetic remarks as these :

" Oh, you willin ! D'you hear that, you wretch ? What
d'you mean by writin' of my grandson in that way ? Take
that, you serpint ! Oh, you wiper, you ! tryin' to break a
lone widder's heart with such scand'lus lies as them !
There, you willin ! I kemmere to hammer you well with
this here umbreller, you owdacious wiper, you ! Take that,
and that, you wile, indecent, disgustin' wagabone ! When
you know well enough that Aleck never had no Uncle Jerry,
and never had no uncle in no sepulchre anyhow, you wile
wretch, you !"

When Mr. Slimmer had concluded his portion of the entertainment, he left the colonel in the hands of the enemy
and fled. He has not been seen in New Castle since that
day, and it is supposed that he has returned to Sussex
county for the purpose of continuing in private his dalli-
ance with the Muses. Colonel Bangs appears to have
abandoned the idea of establishing a department of obitu-
ary poetry, and the *Argus* has resumed its accustomed as-
pect of dreariness.

It may fairly boast, however, that once during its
career it has produced a profound impression upon the
community.

SNYDER'S NOSE.
" OUR FAT CONTRIBUTOR."

Snyder kept a beer-saloon some years ago "over the Rhine." Snyder was a ponderous Teuton of very irascible temper—"sudden and quick in quarrel"—get mad in a minute. Nevertheless, his saloon was a great resort for "the boys"—partly because of the excellence of his beer, and partly because they liked to chafe "old Snyder," as they called him; for, although his bark was terrific, experience had taught them that he wouldn't bite.

One day Snyder was missing; and it was explained by his "frau," who "jerked" the beer that day, that he had "gone out fishing mit der poys." The next day one of the boys, who was particularly fond of "roasting" old Snyder, dropped in to get a glass of beer, and discovered Snyder's nose, which was a big one at any time, swollen and blistered by the sun, until it looked like a dead-ripe tomato.

"Why, Snyder, what's the matter with your nose?" said the caller.

"I peen out fishing mit der poys," replied Snyder, laying his finger tenderly against his proboscis: "the sun it pese hot like ash never vas, and I purns my nose. Nice nose, don't it?" And Snyder viewed it with a look of comical sadness in the little mirror back of his bar. It entered at once into the head of the mischievous fellow in front of the bar to play a joke upon Snyder; so he went out and collected half a dozen of his comrades, with whom he arranged that they should drop in at the saloon one after another, and ask Snyder, "What's the matter with that nose?" to see how long he would stand it. The man who put up the job went in first with a companion, and seating themselves at a table called for beer. Snyder brought it to them; and the new-comer exclaimed as he saw him, "Snyder, what's the matter with your nose?"

"I yust dell your frient here I peen out fishin' mit der

poys, unt de sun he purnt 'em—zwi lager—den cents—all right."

Another boy rushes in. "Halloo, boys, you're ahead of me this time; s'pose I'm in, though. Here, Snyder, bring me a glass of lager and a pret—" (Appears to catch a sudden glimpse of Snyder's nose, looks wonderingly a moment, and then bursts out laughing.) "Ha, ha, ha! Why, Snyder—ha, ha!—what's the matter with that nose?"

Snyder, of course, can't see any fun in having a burnt nose, or having it laughed at; and he says, in a tone sternly emphatic—

"I peen out fishin' mit der poys, unt de sun it yust as hot ash blazes, unt I purnt my nose; dat ish all right."

Another tormentor comes in, and insists on "setting 'em up" for the whole house. "Snyder," says he, "fill up the boys' glasses, and take a drink yourse— Ho, ho, ho, ho! ha, ha, ha! Snyder, wha—ha, ha! what's the matter with that nose?"

Snyder's brow darkens with wrath by this time, and his voice grows deeper and sterner—

"I peen out fishin' mit der poys on the Leedle Miami. De sun pese hot like ash—vel, I purn my pugle. Now, dat is more vot I don't got to say. Vot gind o' peseness? Dat ish all right; I purn my *own* nose, don't it?"

"Burn your nose—burn all the hair off your head, for what I care; you needn't get mad about it."

It was evident that Snyder wouldn't stand more than one more tweak at that nose; for he was tramping about behind the bar, and growling like an exasperated old bear in his cage. Another one of his tormentors walks in. Some one sings out to him, "Have a glass of beer, Billy?"

"Don't care about any beer," says Billy; "but, Snyder, you may give me one of your best ciga— Ha-a-a! ha, ha, ha! ho, ho, ho! he, he, he! ah-h-h-ha! ha, ha, ha! Why— why—Snyder—who—who—ha-ha! ha! what's the matter with that nose?"

Snyder was absolutely fearful to behold by this time; his face was purple with rage, all except his nose, which glowed like a ball of fire. Leaning his ponderous figure far over the bar, and raising his arm aloft to emphasize his words with it, he fairly roared—

"I peen out fishin' mit ter poys. The sun it pese hot like ash never vas. I purnt my nose. Now you no like dose nose, you yust take dose nose unt wr-wr-wr-wring your mean American finger mit 'em! That's the kind of man vot I am!" And Snyder was right.

MAGDALENA, OR THE SPANISH DUEL.
J. F. WALLER.

[NOTE.—The approximately correct pronunciation of the Spanish names may be indicated as follows: *Sevilla*, Seveelya; *Quien Sabe*, Kee-en Sabe (*a* as in father); *Caballero*, Cavalyaro; *Camillo*, Cameelyo; *Miguel*, Migàle; *Pedrillo*, Pedreelyo; *De Xymenes y Ribera*, Da Zimanes e Ribara; *Y Santallos y Herrera*, E Santalyos e Herrara; *Guzman*, Guthman; *Y de Rivas y Mendoza*, E da Reevas e Mendotha; *Y Quintana y de Rosa*, E Keentanya e de Rosas; *Y Zorilla*, E Zoreellya.]

Near the city of Sevilla,
    Years and years ago—
Dwelt a lady in a villa
    Years and years ago;
And her hair was black as night,
And her eyes were starry bright;
Olives on her brow were blooming,
Roses red her lips perfuming,
And her step was light and airy
As the tripping of a fairy;
When she spoke, you thought, each minute,
'Twas the trilling of a linnet;
When she sang, you heard a gush
Of full-voiced sweetness like a thrush
And she struck from the guitar
Ringing music, sweeter far
Than the morning breezes make

Through the lime trees when they shake—
Than the ocean murmuring o'er
Pebbles on the foamy shore.
Orphaned both of sire and mother
    Dwelt she in that lonely villa,
Absent now her guardian brother
    On a mission from Sevilla.
Skills it little now the telling
    How I wooed that maiden fair,
Tracked her to her lonely dwelling
    And obtained an entrance there.
Ah! that lady of the villa—
    And I loved her so,
Near the city of Sevilla,
    Years and years ago.
Ay de mi!—Like echoes falling
    Sweet and sad and low,
Voices come at night, recalling
    Years and years ago.

Once again I'm sitting near thee,
    Beautiful and bright;
Once again I see and hear thee
    In the autumn night ;
Once again I'm whispering to thee
    Faltering words of love;
Once again with song I woo thee
    In the orange grove
Growing near that lonely villa
    Where the waters flow
Down to the city of Sevilla—
    Years and years ago.

'Twas an autumn eve ; the splendor
    Of the day was gone,
And the twilight, soft and tender,
    Stole so gently on
That the eye could scarce discover
How the shadows, spreading over,
    Like a veil of silver gray,

Toned the golden clouds, sun-painted,
Till they paled, and paled, and fainted
   From the face of heaven away.
And a dim light, rising slowly,
   O'er the welkin spread,
Till the blue sky, calm and holy,
   Gleamed above our head;
And the thin moon, newly nascent,
   Shone in glory meek and sweet,
As Murillo paints her crescent
   Underneath Madonna's feet.
And we sat outside the villa
   Where the waters flow
Down to the city of Sevilla—
   Years and years ago.

There we sate—the mighty river
   Wound its serpent course along
Silent, dreamy Guadalquiver,
   Famed in many a song.
Silver gleaming 'mid the plain
   Yellow with the golden grain,
Gliding down through deep, rich meadow
   Where the sated cattle rove,
Stealing underneath the shadows
   Of the verdant olive grove;
With its plenitude of waters,
   Ever flowing calm and slow,
Loved by Andalusia's daughters,
   Sung by poets long ago.

Seated half within a bower
   Where the languid evening breeze
Shook out odors in a shower
   From oranges and citron trees,

Sang she from a romancero,
   How a Moorish chieftain bold
Fought a Spanish caballero
   By Sevilla's walls of old.

How they battled for a lady,
    Fairest of the maids of Spain—
How the Christian's lance, so steady,
    Pierced the Moslem through the brain.

Then she ceased—her black eyes moving, .
    Flashed, as asked she with a smile,
"Say, are maids as fair and loving—
    Men as faithful, in your isle ?"

"British maids," I said, "are ever
    Counted fairest of the fair;
Like the swans on yonder river
    Moving with a stately air.

"Wooed not quickly, won not lightly—
    But, when won, forever true;
Trial draws the bond more tightly,
    Time can ne'er the knot undo."

"And the men ?"—"Ah ! dearest lady,
    Are—quien sabe ? who can say ?
To make love they're ever ready,
    Where they can and where they may;

"Fixed as waves, as breezes steady
    In a changeful April day—
Como brisas, como rios,
    No se sabe, sabe Dios."

"Are they faithful ?"—"Ah ! quien sabe ?
    Who can answer that they are ?
While we may we should be happy."
    Then I took up her guitar,
And I sang in sportive strain,
This song to an old air of Spain.
            "Quien Sabe."

I.

"The breeze of the evening that cools the hot air,
That kisses the orange and shakes out thy hair,
Is its freshness less welcome, less sweet its perfume,
That you know not the region from which it is come ?

Whence the wind blows, where the wind goes,
Hither and thither and whither—who knows?
Who knows?
Hither and thither—but whither—who knows?

II.

"The river forever glides singing along,
The rose on the bank bends down to its song;
And the flower, as it listens, unconsciously dips,
Till the rising wave glistens and kisses its lips.
But why the wave rises and kisses the rose,
And why the rose stoops for those kisses—who knows?
Who knows?
And away flows the river—but whither—who knows?

III.

"Let *me* be the breeze, love, that wanders along
The river that ever rejoices in song;
Be *thou* to my fancy the orange in bloom,
The rose by the river that gives its perfume.
Would the fruit be so golden, so fragrant the rose,
If no breeze and no wave were to kiss them?
Who knows?
Who knows?
If no breeze and no wave were to kiss them?
Who knows?"

As I sang, the lady listened,
Silent save one gentle sigh:
When I ceased, a tear-drop glistened
On the dark fringe of her eye.

Then my heart reproved the feeling
Of that false and heartless strain
Which I sang in words concealing
What my heart would hide in vain.

Up I sprang. What words were uttered
Bootless now to think or tell—
Tongues speak wild when hearts are fluttered
By the mighty master spell.

Love, avowed with sudden boldness,
    Heard with flushings that reveal,
Spite of woman's studied coldness,
    Thoughts the heart cannot conceal.

Words half-vague and passion-broken,
    Meaningless, yet meaning all
That the lips have left unspoken,
    That we never may recall.

"Magdalena, dearest, hear me,"
    Sighed I, as I seized her hand—
"Hola! Senor," very near me,
    Cries a voice of stern command.

And a stalwart caballero
    Comes upon me with a stride,
On his head a slouched sombrero,
    A toledo by his side.

From his breast he flung his capa
    With a stately Spanish air—
[On the whole, he looked the chap a
    Man to slight would scarcely dare.]

"Will your worship have the goodness
    To release that lady's hand ?"
"Senor," I replied, "this rudeness
    I am not prepared to stand.

"Magdalena, say "—the maiden,
    With a cry of wild surprise,
As with secret sorrow laden,
    Fainting sank before my eyes.

Then the Spanish caballero
    Bowed with haughty courtesy,
Solemn as a tragic hero,
    And announced himself to me.

        "Senor, I am Don Camillo
        Guzman Miguel Pedrillo
        De Xymenes y Ribera
        Y Santallos y Herrera

Y de Rivas y Mendoza
Y Quintana y de Rosa
Y Zorilla y "—" No more, sir,
'Tis as good as twenty score, sir,"
Said I to him, with a frown;
" Mucha bulla para nada,
No palabras, draw your 'spada;
If you're up for a duello
You will find I'm just your fellow—
Senor, I am Peter Brown !"

By the river's brink that night,
    Foot to foot in strife,
Fought we in the dubious light
    A fight of death or life.
Don Camillo slashed my shoulder,
With the pain I grew the bolder,
    Close, and closer still I pressed;
Fortune favored me at last,
I broke his guard, my weapon passed
    Through the caballero's breast—

Down to the earth went Don Camillo
Guzman Miguel Pedrillo
De Xymenes y Ribera
Y Santallos y Herrera
Y de Rivas y Mendoza
Y Quintana y de Rosa
Y Zorilla y—   One groan,
And he lay motionless as stone.
The man of many names went down,
Pierced by the sword of Peter Brown !

Kneeling down, I raised his head;
The cabellero faintly said,
" Senor Ingles, fly from Spain
With all speed, for you have slain
A Spanish noble, Don Camillo
Guzman Miguel Pedrillo
De Xymenes y Ribera
Y Santallos y Herrera

Y de Rivas y Mendoza
Y Quintana y de Rosa
Y Zorilla y "— He swooned
With the bleeding from his wound.
If he be living still, or dead,
    I never knew, I ne'er shall know.
That night from Spain in haste I fled,
    Years and years ago.

Oft when autumn eve is closing,
    Pensive, puffing a cigar,
In my chamber lone reposing,
Musing half, and half a-dozing,
    Comes a vision from afar
Of that lady of the villa
In her satin, fringed mantilla,
And that haughty caballero
With his capa and sombrero,
Vainly in my mind revolving
    That long, jointed, endless name ;—
'Tis a riddle past my solving,
    Who he was or whence he came.
Was he that brother home returned ?
Was he some former lover spurned ?
Or some family *fiance*
That the lady did not fancy ?
Was he any one of those ?
Sabe Dios. Ah, God knows!

Sadly smoking my manilla,
    Much I long to know
How fares the lady of the villa
    That once charmed me so,
When I visited Sevilla
    Years and years ago.
Has she married a Hidalgo ?
Gone the way that ladies all go
In those drowsy Spanish cities,
Wasting life—a thousand pities—
Waking up for a fiesta

From an afternoon siesta,
To " Giralda " now repairing,
Or the Plaza for an airing;
At the shaded *reja* flirting,
At a bull fight now desporting;
Does she walk at evenings ever
Through the gardens by the river ?
Guarded by an old duenna
Fierce and sharp as a hyena,
With her goggles and her fan
Warning off each wicked man ?
Is she dead or is she living ?
Is she for my absence grieving ?
Is she wretched, is she happy ?
Widow, wife, or maid ?   *Quien sabe ?*

"BAY BILLY."

FRANK H. GASSAWAY.

'Twas the last fight at Fredericksburg—
    Perhaps the day you reck,
Our boys, the Twenty-Second Maine,
    Kept Early's men in check.
Just where Wade Hampton boomed away
    The fight went neck and neck.

All day we held the weaker wing,
    And held it with a will;
Five several stubborn times we charged
    The battery on the hill,
And five times beaten back, reformed,
    And kept our columns still.

At last from out the centre fight
    Spurred up a General's Aid.
" That battery *must* silenced be !"
    He cried, as past he sped.
Our Colonel simply touched his cap,
    And then, with measured tread,

To lead the crouching line once more
  The grand old fellow came.
No wounded man but raised his head
  And strove to gasp his name,
And those who could not speak nor stir,
  "God blessed him " just the same.

For he was all the world to us,
  That hero gray and grim ;
Right well he knew that fearful slope
  We'd climb with none but him,
Though while his white head led the way
  We'd charge hell's portals in.

This time we were not half way up,
  When, midst the storm of shell,
Our leader, with his sword upraised,
  Beneath our bay'nets fell.
And, as we bore him back, the foe
  Set up a joyous yell.

Our hearts went with him. Back we swept,
  And when the bugle said
"Up, charge, again !" no man was there
  But hung his dogged head.
"We've no one left to lead us now,"
  The sullen soldiers said.

Just then, before the laggard line
  The Colonel's horse we spied—
Bay Billy with his trappings on,
  His nostril swelling wide,
As though still on his gallant back
  The master sat astride.

Right royally he took the place
  That was of old his wont,
And with a neigh, that seemed to say
  Above the battle's brunt,
"How can the Twenty-Second charge
  If I am not in front ?"

Like statues we stood rooted there,
    And gazed a little space ;
Above that floating mane we missed
    The dear familiar face ;
But we saw Bay Billy's eye of fire,
    And it gave us heart of grace.

No bugle call could rouse us all
    As that brave sight had done ;
Down all the battered line we felt
    A lightning impulse run ;
Up, up the hill we followed Bill,
    And captured every gun !

And when upon the conquered height
    Died out the battle's hum,
Vainly 'mid living and the dead
    We sought our leader dumb ;
It seemed as if a spectre steed
    To win that day had come.

At last the morning broke.   The lark
    Sang in the merry skies
As if to e'en the sleepers there
    It bade wake, and arise !
Though naught but that last trump of all
    Could ope their heavy eyes.

And then once more, with banners gay,
    Stretched out the long brigade ;
Trimly upon the furrowed field
    The troops stood on parade,
And bravely 'mid the ranks were closed
    The gaps the fight had made.

Not half the Twenty-Second's men
    Were in their place that morn,
And Corp'ral Dick, who yester-noon
    Stood six brave fellows on,
Now touched my elbow in the ranks,
    For all between were gone.

Ah! who forgets that dreary hour
    When, as with misty eyes,
To call the old familiar roll
    The solemn Sergeant tries—
One feels that thumping of the heart
    As no prompt voice replies.

And as in falt'ring tone and slow
    The last few names were said,
Across the field some missing horse
    Toiled up with weary tread.
It caught the Sergeant's eye, and quick
    Bay Billy's name was read.

Yes! there the old bay hero stood,
    All safe from battle's harms,
And ere an order could be heard,
    Or the bugle's quick alarms,
Down all the front, from end to end,
    The troops presented arms!

Not all the shoulder-straps on earth
    Could still our mighty cheer.
And ever from that famous day,
    When rang the roll-call clear,
Bay Billy's name was read, and then
    The whole line answered " Here!"

RETURN OF THE HILLSIDE LEGION.
ETHEL LYNN.

What telegraphed word
    The village hath stirred ?
Why eagerly gather the people ;
    And why do they wait
    At crossing and gate—
Why flutters the flag on the steeple ?

        Why, stranger, do tell—
        It's now a smart spell

Since our sogers went marchin' away,
And we calculate now
To show the boys how
We can welcome the Legion to-day.

Bill Allendale's drum
Will sound when they come,
And there's watchers above on the hill,
To let us all know
When the big bugles blow,
To hurrah with a hearty good will.

All the women folks wait
By the 'Cademy gate,
With posies all drippin' with dew;
The Legion shan't say
We helped them away,
And forgot them when service was through.

My Jack's comin' too,
He's served the war through;
Hark, the rattle and roar of the train!
There's bugle and drum,
Our sogers have come!
Hurrah! for the boys home again.

"Stand aside! stand aside!
Leave a space far and wide
Till the regiment forms on the track."
Two soldiers in blue,
Two men—only two
Stepped off, and the Legion was back.

The hurrah softly died
In the space far and wide,
As they welcomed the worn, weary men;
The drum on the hill
Grew suddenly still,
And the bugle was silent again.

I asked Farmer Shore
A question no more,

For a sick soldier lay on his breast!
While his hand, hard and brown,
Stroked tenderly down
The locks of the weary at rest.

CUDDLE DOON.
ALEXANDER ANDERSON

The bairnies cuddle doon at nicht
Wi' muckle faucht an' din.
"Oh, try and sleep, ye waukrife rogues:
Your father's comin' in."
They never heed a word I speak.
I try to gie a froon;
But aye I hap them up, an' cry,
"Oh, bairnies, cuddle doon!"

Wee Jamie wi' the curly heid—
He aye sleeps next the wa'—
Bangs up an' cries, "I want a piece"—
The rascal starts them a'.
I rin an' fetch them pieces, drinks—
They stop awee the soun'—
Then draw the blankets up, and cry,
"Noo, weanies, cuddle doon!"

But ere five minutes gang, wee Rab
Cries oot, frae 'neath the claes,
"Mither, mak' Tam gie ower at ance:
He's kittlin' wi' his taes."
The mischief's in that Tam for tricks:
He'd bother half the toon.
But aye I hap them up, and cry,
"Oh, bairnies cuddle doon!"

At length they hear their father's fit;
An' as he steeks the door,
They turn their faces to the wa',
While Tam pretends to snore.

"Hae a' the weans been gude ?" he asks,
    As he pits aff his shoon.
"The bairnies, John, are in their beds,
    An' lang since cuddled doon."

An' just afore we bed oorsels,
    We look at oor wee lambs.
Tam has his airm roun' wee Rab's neck,
    An' Rab his airm roun' Tam's.
I lift wee Jamie up the bed,
    An' as I straik each croon,
I whisper, till my heart fills up,
    "Oh, bairnies, cuddle doon !"

The bairnies cuddle doon at nicht
    Wi' mirth that's dear to me ;
But soon the big warl's cark an' care
    Will quaten doon their glee.
Yet, come what will to ilka ane,
    May He who sits aboon
Aye whisper, though their pows be bauld,
    "Oh, bairnies, cuddle doon !"

SHERIDAN'S RIDE.

THOMAS BUCHANAN READ.

Up from the South at break of day,
Bringing to Winchester fresh dismay,
The affrighted air with a shudder bore,
Like a herald in haste to the chieftain's door,
The terrible grumble, and rumble, and roar,
Telling the battle was on once more,
And Sheridan twenty miles away.

And wider still those billows of war
Thundered along the horizon's bar ;
And louder yet into Winchester rolled
The roar of that red sea uncontrolled,
Making the blood of the listener cold,

As he thought of the stake in that fiery fray,
And Sheridan twenty miles away.

But there is a road from Winchester town,
A good broad highway leading down;
And there, through the flush of the morning light,
A steed as black as the steeds of night
Was seen to pass, as with eagle flight
As if he knew the terrible need;
He stretched away with his utmost speed;
Hills rose and fell; but his heart was gay,
With Sheridan fifteen miles away.

Still sprung from those swift hoofs, thundering South,
The dust, like smoke from the cannon's mouth;
Or the trail of a comet, sweeping faster and faster,
Foreboding to traitors the doom of disaster.
The heart of the steed, and the heart of the master
Were beating like prisoners assaulting their walls,
Impatient to be where the battle-field calls;
Every nerve of the charger was strained to full play,
With Sheridan only ten miles away.

Under his spurning feet, the road
Like an arrowy Alpine river flowed,
And the landscape sped away behind
Like an ocean flying before the wind,
And the steed, like a bark fed with furnace ire,
Swept on, with his wild eye full of fire.
But lo! he is nearing his heart's desire ;
He is snuffing the smoke of the roaring fray,
With Sheridan only five miles away.

The first that the General saw were the groups
Of stragglers, and then the retreating troops;
What was done? what to do? a glance told him both;
Then striking his spurs, with a terrible oath
He dashed down the line, 'mid a storm of huzzas,
And the wave of retreat checked its course there, because
The sight of the master compelled it to pause.
With foam and with dust the black charger was gray;

By the flash of his eye, and the red nostril's play,
He seemed to the whole great army to say,
" I have brought you Sheridan all the way
From Winchester, down to save the day."

Hurrah! hurrah for Sheridan!
Hurrah! hurrah for horse and man!
And when their statues are placed on high
Under the dome of the Union sky,
The American soldiers' Temple of Fame,
There with the glorious General's name
Be it said in letters both bold and bright:
" Here is the steed that saved the day
By carrying Sheridan into the fight,
From Winchester—twenty miles away!"

THE POWER OF PRAYER:
OR, THE FIRST STEAMBOAT UP THE ALABAMA.
From   eribner's Magazine.

You, Dinah! Come and set me whar de ribber-roads does meet.
De Lord, *He* made dese black-jack roots to twis' into a seat.
Umph, dar! De Lord have mussy on dis blin' ole nigger's feet.

It 'pear to me dis mornin' I kin smell de fust o' June.
I 'clar', I b'lieve dat mocking-bird could play de fiddle soon!
Dem yonder town-bells sounds like dey was ringin' in de moon.

Well, if dis nigger *is* been blind for fo'ty year or mo',
Dese ears, *dey* sees the world, like, th'u' de cracks dat's in de do',
For de Lord has built dis body wid de windows 'hind and 'fo'.

I know my front ones *is* stopped up, and things is sort o' dim,
But den, th'u' *dem*, temptation's rain won't leak in on ole Jim!
De back ones shows me earth enough, aldo' dey's mons'ous slim.

And as for Hebben—bless de Lord, and praise His holy name—
Dat shines in all de co'ners of dis cabin jes' de same
As ef dat cabin hadn't nar' a plank upon de frame!

Who *call* me ? Listen down de ribber, Dinah ! Don't you hyar
Somebody holl'in' *" hoo, Jim, hoo" ?* My Sarah died las' y'ar;
Is dat black angel done come back to call ole Jim f'om hyar ?

My stars, dat cain't be Sarah, shuh ! Jes' listen, Dinah, *now !*
What *kin* be comin' up dat bend, a-makin' sich a row ?
Fus' bellerin' like a pawin' bull, den squealin' like a sow ?

De Lord 'a' massy sakes alive, jes' hear—ker-woof, ker-woof—
De Debble's comin' round dat bend, he's comin', shuh enuff,
A-splashin' up de water wid his tail and wid his hoof !

I'se pow'ful skeered ; but neversomeless, I ain't gwine run away ;
I'm gwine to stand stiff-legged for de Lord dis blessed day.
You screech, and howl, and swish de water, Satan ! Let us pray.

O hebbenly Mah'sr, what Thou willest, dat mus' be jes' so,
And ef Thou hast bespoke de word, some nigger's bound to go.
Den, Lord, please take ole Jim, and lef young Dinah hyar below !

Scuse Dinah, scuse her, Mah'sr ; for she's sich a little chile,
She hardly jes' begin to scramble up de home-yard stile,
But dis ole traveler's feet been tired dis many a many a mile.

I'se wufless as de rotten pole of las' year's fodder-stack.
De rheumatiz done bit my bones ; you hear 'em crack and crack ?
I cain't sit down 'dout gruntin' like 'twas breakin' o' my back.

What use de wheel, when hub and spokes is warped and split and
    rotten ?
What use dis dried-up cotton-stalk, when Life done picked my
    cotton ?
I'se like a word dat somebody done said, and den forgotten.

But, Dinah ! Shuh dat gal jes' like dis little hick'ry-tree,
De sap's jes' risin' in her ; she do grow owdaciouslee—
Lord, ef you's cl'arin' de underbrush, don't cut her down, cut me !

I would not proud persume—but yet I'll boldly make reques' ;
Sence Jacob had dat wrastlin'-match, I, too, gwine do my bes' ;
When Jacob got all underholt, de Lord He answered Yes !

And what for waste de vittles, now, and th'ow away de bread,
Jes' for to strength dese idle hands to scratch dis ole bald head ?
T'ink of de 'conomy, Mah'sr, if dis ole Jim was dead !

Stop! ef I don't believe de Debble's gone on up de stream!
Jes' now he squealed down dar—hush! dat's a mighty weakly
  scream!
Yas, sir, he's gone, he's gone! he snort 'way off, like in a dream!

O glory hallelujah to de Lord dat reigns on high!
De Debble's fa'ly skeered to def, he done gone flyin' by;
I know'd he couldn't stand dat pra'r, I felt my Mah'sr nigh!

You, Dinah; ain't you 'shamed, now, dat you didn' trust to grace?
I heerd you thrashin' th'u' de bushes when he showed his face!
You fool, you think de Debble couldn't beat *you* in a race?

I tell you, Dinah, jes' as sure as you is standin' dar,
When folks starts prayin', answer-angels drops down th'u' de a'r.
Yea, Dinah, whar 'ould you be now, exceptin' for dat pra'r?

HOWARD'S RECITATIONS.

Comic, Serious and Pathetic. Being a carefully selected collection of fresh Recitations in Prose and Poetry, suitable for Anniversaries, Exhibitions, Social Gatherings, and Evening Parties; affording, also, an abundance of excellent material for practice and declamation. Edited by Clarence J. Howard.

CONTENTS.

16mo. 180 pages. Paper covers. Price.............................30 cts.
Bound in boards, cloth back... ....50 cts.

BEECHER'S RECITATIONS
AND
READINGS.

Humorous, Serious, Dramatic, including Prose and Poetical Selections in Dutch, French, Yankee, Irish, Backwoods, Negro and other Dialects. Edited by Alvah C. Beecher. This excellent selection has been compiled to meet a growing demand for Public Readings, and contains a number of the favorite pieces that have been rendered with telling effect by the most popular Public Readers of the present time. It includes, also, choice selections for Recitations, and is, therefore, admirably adapted for use at Evening Entertainments, School Celebrations, and other Festival occasions.

CONTENTS.

Paper covers. Price.....................................30 cts.
Bound in boards, cloth back.....................................50 cts.

Kavauaugh's Juvenile Speaker. For very little boys and

girls. Containing short and easily-learned Speeches and Dialogues, expressly adapted for School Celebrations, May-Day Festivals and other Children's Entertainments. By Mrs. Russell Kavanaugh. This book is just the thing for Teachers, as it gives a great number of short pieces for very young children, with directions for appropriate dresses.

It includes a complete programme for a May-Day Festival, with opening chorus and appropriate speeches for nineteen boys and girls, including nearly forty additional speeches for young and very small children.

It introduces the May-Pole Dance, plainly described in every detail, and forming a very attractive and pleasing exhibition.

Besides the above, it contains the following Dialogues and Recitations, for two, three or more boys and girls of various ages:

	Boys.	Girls		Boys.	Girls
Salutatory	1		Balance Due	1	
Salutatory	1		Recitation	1	
Opening Song		13	The Coming Woman	1	
Opening Recitation	1	12	Speech		1
An Interrupted Recitation	1	1	The Power of Temper	1	
An Imaginative Invention	1		Truth and Falsehood	1	
Speech		1	Recitation		1
A Joyful Surprise	3	2	Recitation	1	
An Oration	1		Recitation	1	
How He Had Him	2	1	Christmas Forty Years Ago	1	
The Old Maid		1	Speech		1
The Old Bachelor	1		Trying Hard	1	
Poetry, Prose and Fact	1	2	The School-Boy	1	
The Dumb Wife	1		Recitation		1
To Inconsistent Husbands	1		"I Told You So"	1	
Small Pitchers have Large Ears		2	Speech	1	
Sour Grapes	1		Speech		1
Not Worth While to Hate	1		Choosing a Name		1
A Strike Among the Flowers		1	Baby Bye		4
A Witty Retort	1		Dialogue	2	
The Young Critic	2		Little Puss		1
"They Say"		1	Poor Men vs. Rich Men	1	
Speech	1		Helping Papa and Mamma	2	2
"Angels Can Do No More."	1		Annabel's First Party		1
Recitation	1		The Spendthrift Doll		1
Dialogue	1	1	The Little Mushrooms		3
Holiday Speech	1		Valedictory	1	
The Love-Scrape	2	1	Riding in the Cars		1
An Old Ballad	1	1	Riding in the Cars	1	
The Milkmaid	1	1	Speech	1	
Billy Grimes, the Drover		2	The Cobbler's Secret	1	
Grandmother's Beau		1	Dialogue	1	1
Speech	1		Valedictory	1	
Honesty the Best Policy	4				

The whole embraces a hundred and twenty-three easy and very effective pieces, from which selections can be made to suit the capacities of boys and girls of from two to sixteen years of age.

16mo, illuminated paper cover. Price.................................30 cts.
"   Boards ....50 cts.

WILSON'S BOOK OF RECITATIONS
AND
DIALOGUES.

With instructions in Elocution and Declamation. Containing a choice selection of Poetical and Prose Recitations. Designed as an Assistant to Teachers and Students in preparing Exhibitions. By Floyd B. Wilson, Professor of Elocution.

CONTENTS.

Paper covers. Price...30 cts.
Bound in boards, cloth back,.......................................50 cts

BARTON'S COMIC RECITATIONS

AND

HUMOROUS DIALOGUES.

Containing a variety of Comic Recitations in Prose and Poetry, Amusing Dialogues, Burlesque Scenes, Eccentric Orations, Humorous Interludes and Laughable Farces. Designed for School Commencements and Amateur Theatricals. Edited by Jerome Barton.

CONTENTS.

This is one of the best collection of Humorous Pieces especially adapted to the Parlor Stage that has ever been published. 16 mo. 180 pages.

Paper covers. Price ....**30 cts.**

Bound in boards, cloth back......................... • ....**50 cts.**

SPENCER'S BOOK OF COMIC SPEECHES
AND
HUMOROUS RECITATIONS.

A collection of Comic Speeches and Dialogues, Humorous Prose and Poetical Recitations, Laughable Dramatic Scenes and Burlesques, and Eccentric Characteristic Soliloquies and Stories. Suitable for School Exhibitions and Evening Entertainments. Edited by Albert J. Spencer.

CONTENTS.

Paper covers. Price..**30 cts.**

Bound in boards, cloth back...**50 cts.**

BRUDDER BONES' BOOK OF STUMP SPEECHES

AND

BURLESQUE ORATIONS.

Also containing Humorous Lectures, Ethiopian Dialogues, Plantation Scenes, Negro Farces and Burlesques, Laughable interludes and Comic Recitations. Compiled and edited by John F. Scott.

CONTENTS.

16 mo. 188 pages. Paper covers. Price ....30 cts.
Bound in boards, illuminated: ....50 cts.

MARTINE'S DROLL DIALOGUES

AND

LAUGHABLE RECITATIONS.

By Arthur Martine, author of "Martine's Letter-Writer," etc., etc. A collection of Humorous Dialogues, Comic Recitations, Brilliant Burlesque, Spirited Stump Speeches and Ludicrous Farces, adapted for School and other Celebrations and for Home Amusement.

CONTENTS.

188 pages. Paper covers. Price.....................................30 cts.

Bound in boards, cloth back... ....50 cts.

Frost's Dialogues for Young Folks. A Collection of Original, Moral and Humorous Dialogues. Adapted to the use of School and Church Exhibitions, Family Gatherings and Juvenile Celebrations on all Occasions. By S. A. Frost.

CONTENTS.	Boys.	Girls.	CONTENTS.	Boys.	Girls.
Novel Reading	1	1	A Place for Everything	2	2
The Bound Girl		4	I Want to be a Soldier	2	
Writing a Letter		2	Self-Denial	2	3
The Wonderful Scholar	1	2	The Traveler	3	
Slang	4		Idleness the Mother of Evil		4
The Language of Flowers		4	The French Lesson	5	
The Morning Call		4	Civility Never Lost	3	2
The Spoiled Child		4	Who Works the Hardest?	1	1
The Little Travelers	2	2	The Everlasting Talker		5
Little Things	1	1	The Epicure	3	
Generosity		2	True Charity	1	-
Country Cousins		4	Starting in Life	1	1
Winning the Prize		2	I Didn't Mean Anything	4	
The Unfortunate Scholar		4	Ambition	5	
The Day of Misfortunes	3		Choosing a Trade	9	
Jealousy	1	3	The Schoolmaster Abroad	7	
The May Queen		5	White Lies	3	
Temptation Resisted	3		The Hoyden	1	3

16mo, Paper Covers. Price...30 cts.
Bound in Boards...50 cts.

Frost's New Book of Dialogues. A series of entirely new and original humorous Dialogues, specially adapted for performance at School Anniversaries and Exhibitions, or other Festivals and Celebrations of the Young Folks.

CONTENTS.	Boys.	Girls.	CONTENTS.	Boys.	Girls.
Slang versus Dictionary	3		The Intelligence Office	4	3
Country or City		3	Cats	6	
Turning the Tables	3		Too Fine and Too Plain		3
The Force of Imagination		4	The Fourth of July Oration	5	
The Modern Robinson Crusoe	5		The Sewing Circle		7
The Threatened Visit		3	Fix	2	
The Dandy and the Boor	3		The Yankee Aunt	2	3
Nature versus Education		4	The Walking Encyclopedia	5	
The British Lion and American Hoosier	3		The Novel Readers		3
			The Model Farmer	2	
Curing a Pedant		5	Buying a Sewing-Machine	4	2
Pursuit of Knowledge under Difficulties	2		Sam Weller's Valentine	2	
			The Hungry Traveler	2	
The Daily Governess		2	Deaf as a Post	1	2
The Army and Navy	2	2	The Rehearsal	6	
Economy is Wealth		3			

These Dialogues are admirably adapted for home performance, as they require no set scenery for their representation. By S. A. Frost. 180 pages, 16mo.

Paper covers. Price...30 cts.
Bound in boards, cloth back...50 cts.

CHECKERS AND CHESS.

Spayth's American Draught Player; or, The Theory and Practice of the Scientific Game of Checkers. Simplified and Illustrated with Practical Diagrams. Containing upwards of 1,700 Games and Positions. By Henry Spayth. Sixth edition, with over three hundred Corrections and Improvements. Containing: The Standard Laws of the Game— Full instructions—Draught Board Numbered—Names of the Games, and how formed—The "Theory of the Move and its Changes" practically explained and illustrated with Diagrams—Playing Tables for Draught Clubs— New Systems of numbering the Board—Prefixing signs to the Variations— List of Draught Treatises and Publications chronologically arranged. Bound in cloth, gilt side and back............................ ....**$3.00**

Spayth's Game of Draughts. By Henry Spayth. This book is designed as a supplement to the author's first work, "The American Draught Player"; but it is complete in itself. It contains lucid instructions for beginners, laws of the game, diagrams, the score of 304 games, together with 34 novel, instructive and ingenious "critical positions." Cloth, gilt back and side...**$1.50**

Spayth's Draughts or Checkers for Beginners. This treatise was written by Henry Spayth, the celebrated player, and is by far the most complete and instructive elementary work on Draughts ever published. It is profusely illustrated with diagrams of ingenious stratagems, curious positions and perplexing problems, and contains a great variety of interesting and instructive Games, progressively arranged and clearly explained with notes, so that the learner may easily comprehend them. With the aid of this Manual a beginner may soon become a proficient in the game. Cloth, gilt side...**75 cts.**

Scattergood's Game of Draughts, or Checkers, Simplified and Explained. With practical Diagrams and Illustrations, together with a Checker-Board, numbered and printed in red. Containing the Eighteen Standard Games, with over 200 of the best variations, selected from various authors, with some never before published. By D. Scattergood. Bound in cloth, with flexible covers.................................**50 cts.**

Marache's Manual of Chess. Containing a description of the Board and Pieces, Chess Notation, Technical Terms, with diagrams illustrating them, Laws of the Game, Relative Value of Pieces, Preliminary Games for Beginners, Fifty Openings of Games, giving all the latest discoveries of Modern Masters, with the best games and copious notes. Twenty Endings of Games, showing easiest ways of effecting Checkmate. Thirty-six ingenious Diagram Problems, and sixteen curious Chess Stratagems, being one of the best Books for Beginners ever published. By N. Marache. Bound in boards, cloth back...**50 cts.** Bound in cloth, gilt side..**75 cts.**

DICK & FITZGERALD, Publishers,

Box 2975.   NEW YORK.

READINGS AND RECITATIONS.

Kavanaugh's Juvenile Speaker. For very Little Boys
and Girls. Containing short and easily-learned Speeches and Dialogues, expressly adapted for School Celebrations, May-Day Festivals and other Children's Entertainments. Embracing one hundred and twenty-three effective pieces. By Mrs. Russell Kavanaugh. Illuminated paper cover..30 cts.
Bound in boards, cloth back.... ....50 cts.

Dick's Series of Recitations and Readings, Nos. 1 to 7. Comprising a carefully compiled selection of Humorous, Pathetic, Eloquent, Patriotic and Sentimental Pieces in Poetry and Prose, exclusively designed for Recitation or Reading. Edited by Wm. B Dick. Each number of the Series contains about 180 pages. Illus in red paper cover, each....30 cts.
Bound in full cloth.... ....50 cts.

Beecher's Recitations and Readings. Humorous, Serious, Dramatic, including Prose and Poetical Selections in Dutch, Yankee, Irish, Negro and other Dialects. 180 pages, paper covers........ ......30 cts.
Bound in boards, cloth back................................50 cts.

Howard's Recitations. Comic, Serious and Pathetic. Being a collection of fresh Recitations in Prose and Poetry, suitable for Exhibitions and Evening Parties. 180 pages, paper covers........ ......30 cts.
Bound in boards, cloth back................................50 cts.

Spencer's Book of Comic Speeches and Humorous Recitations. A collection of Comic Speeches, Humorous Prose and Poetical Recitations, Laughable Dramatic Scenes and Eccentric Dialect Stories.
192 pages, paper covers. ....30 cts.
Bound in boards, cloth back................................50 cts.

Wilson's Book of Recitations and Dialogues. Containing a choice selection of Poetical and Prose Recitations. Designed as an Assistant to Teachers and Students in preparing Exhibitions.
188 pages, paper covers ....30 cts.
Bound in boards, with cloth back................................50 cts.

Barton's Comic Recitations and Humorous Dialogues. A variety of Comic Recitations in Prose and Poetry, Eccentric Orations and Laughable Interludes. 180 pages, paper covers............ ....30 cts.
Bound in boards, with cloth back................................50 cts.

Brudder Bones' Book of Stump Speeches and Burlesque Orations. Also containing Humorous Lectures, Ethiopian Dialogues, Plantation Scenes. Negro Farces and Burlesques, Laughable Interludes and Comic Recitations. 188 pages, paper covers......................30 cts.
Bound in boards, illuminated................................50 cts.

Martine's Droll Dialogues and Laughable Recitations. A collection of Humorous Dialogues, Comic Recitations, Brilliant Burlesques and Spirited Stump Speeches. 188 pages, paper covers............30 cts.
Bound in boards, with cloth back................................50 cts.

WE WILL SEND A CATALOGUE containing a complete list of all the pieces in each of the above books, to any person who will send us their address. Send for one.

DICK & FITZGERALD, Publishers,
Box 2975. · NEW YORK.

DIALOGUE BOOKS.

*The Dialogues contained in these books are all entirely original;
some of them being arranged for one sex only, and others for
both sexes combined.* They develop in a marked degree the ec-
centricities and peculiarities of the various characters which are
represented in them; and are specially adapted for School Exhibitions and other celebrations, which mainly depend upon the
efforts of the young folks.

McBride's Comic Dialogues. A collection of twenty-three
Original Humorous Dialogues, especially designed for the display of Amateur dramatic talent, and introducing a variety of sentimental, sprightly,
comic and genuine Yankee characters, and other ingeniously developed eccen-
tricities. By H. Elliott McBride. 180 pages, illuminated paper covers..30 cts.
Bound in boards..50 cts.

McBride's All Kinds of Dialogues. A collection of twenty-
five Original, Humorous and Domestic Dialogues, introducing Yankee,
Irish, Dutch and other characters. Excellently adapted for Amateur Performances. 180 pages, illuminated paper covers...................30 cts.
Bound in boards...50 cts.

Holmes' Very Little Dialogues for Very Little Folks. Containing forty-seven New and Original Dialogues, with short and easy parts,
almost entirely in words of one syllable, suited to the capacity and comprehension of very young children. Paper covers......................30 cts.
Bound in boards, cloth back...50 cts.

Frost's Dialogues for Young Folks. A collection of thirty-
six Original, Moral and Humorous Dialogues. Adapted for boys and girls
between the ages of ten and fourteen years. By S. A. Frost.
176 pages, paper covers..30 cts.
Bound in boards.......................... ....50 cts.

Frost's New Book of Dialogues. Containing twenty-nine entirely New and Original Humorous Dialogues for boys and girls between the
ages of twelve and fifteen years. 180 pages, paper covers..........30 cts.
Bound in boards, cloth back........... ....50 cts.

Frost's Humorous and Exhibition Dialogues. This is a collection of twenty-five Sprightly Original Dialogues, in Prose and Verse, intended to be spoken at School Exhibitions. 178 pages, paper covers.30 cts.
Bound in boards...50 cts.

*WE WILL SEND A CATALOGUE free to any address, con-
taining a list of all the Dialogues in each of the above books,
together with the number of boys and girls required to perform
them.*

DICK & FITZGERALD, Publishers,

Box 2975.   NEW YORK.

AMATEUR THEATRICALS.

All the plays in the following excellent books are especially designed for Amateur performance. The majority of them are in one act and one scene, and may be represented in any moderate-sized parlor, without much preparation of costume or scenery.

Burton's Amateur Actor. A complete guide to Private Theatricals; giving plain directions for arranging, decorating and lighting the Stage; with rules and suggestions for mounting, rehearsing and performing all kinds of Plays, Parlor Pantomimes and Shadow Pantomimes. Illustrated with numerous engravings, and including a selection of original Plays, with Prologues, Epilogues, etc. 16mo, illuminated paper cover.....**30 cts.**
Bound in boards, with cloth back..................**50 cts.**

Parlor Theatricals; or, Winter Evenings' Entertainment. Containing Acting Proverbs, Dramatic Charades, Drawing-Room Pantomimes, a Musical Burlesque and an amusing Farce, with instructions for Amateurs. Illustrated with engravings. Paper covers..........**30 cts.**
Bound in boards, cloth back....... .. ..**50 cts.**

Howard's Book of Drawing-Room Theatricals. A collection of twelve short and amusing plays. Some of the plays are adapted for performers of one sex only. 186 pages, paper covers..............**30 cts.**
Bound in boards, with cloth back...........................**50 cts.**

Hudson's Private Theatricals. A collection of fourteen humorous plays. Four of these plays are adapted for performance by males only, and three are for females. 180 pages, paper covers.................**30 cts**
Bound in boards, with cloth back.........................**50 cts.**

Nugent's Burlesque and Musical Acting Charades. Containing ten Charades, all in different styles, two of which are easy and effective Comic Parlor Operas, with Music and Piano-forte Accompaniments. 176 pages, paper covers.............................**30 cts.**
Bound in boards, cloth back...........................**50 cts.**

Frost's Dramatic Proverbs and Charades. Containing eleven Proverbs and fifteen Charades, some of which are for Dramatic Performance, and others arranged for Tableaux Vivants. 176 pages, paper covers.**30 cts.**
Bound in boards, with cloth back............. ....**50 cts.**

Frost's Parlor Acting Charades. These twelve excellent and original Charades are arranged as short parlor Comedies and Farces, full of brilliant repartee and amusing situations. 182 pages, paper covers..**30 cts.**
Illuminated boards.......................**50 cts.**

Frost's Book of Tableaux and Shadow Pantomimes. A collection of Tableaux Vivants and Shadow Pantomimes, with stage instructions for Costuming, Grouping, etc. 180 pages, paper covers..**30 cts.**
Bound in boards, with cloth back............................**50 cts.**

Frost's Amateur Theatricals. A collection of eight original plays; all short, amusing and new. 180 pages, paper covers......**30 cts.**
Bound in boards, with cloth back............................**50 cts.**

WE WILL SEND A CATALOGUE containing a complete list of all the pieces in each of the above books, together with the number of male and female characters in each play, to any person who will send us their address. Send for one.

DICK & FITZGERALD, Publishers,
Box 2975.   NEW YORK.

Mrs. Partington's Carpet-Bag of Fun. A collection of over
1,000 of the most Comical Stories, Amusing Adventures, Side-Splitting
Jokes, Cheek-extending Poetry, Funny Conundrums, Queer Sayings of
Mrs. Partington, Heart-Rending Puns, Witty Repartees, etc. The whole
illustrated by about 150 comic wood-cuts.
12mo, 300 pages, ornamented paper covers......................75 cts.

Harp of a Thousand Strings; or, Laughter for a Life-time.
A book of nearly 400 pages; bound in a handsome gilt cover; crowded full
of funny stories, besides being illustrated with over 200 comic engravings,
by Darley, McLennan, Bellew, etc............ ....$1.50

Chips from Uncle Sam's Jack-Knife. Illustrated with over
100 Comical Engravings, and comprising a collection of over 500 Laughable
Stories, Funny Adventures. Comic Poetry, Queer Conundrums, Territic
Puns and Sentimental Sentences. Large octavo..................25 cts.

Fox's Ethiopian Comicalities. Containing Strange Sayings,
Eccentric Doings, Burlesque Speeches, Laughable Drolleries and Funny
Stories, as recited by the celebrated Ethiopian Comedian............10 cts.

Ned Turner's Circus Joke Book. A collection of the best
Jokes, Bon Mots, Repartees, Gems of Wit and Funny Sayings and Doings
of the celebrated Equestrian Clown and Ethiopian Comedian, Ned Turner...10 cts.

Ned Turner's Black Jokes. A collection of Funny Stories,
Jokes and Conundrums, interspersed with Witty Sayings and Humorous
Dialogues, as given by Ned Turner, the celebrated Ethiopian Delinea-
tor..10 cts.

Ned Turner's Clown Joke Book. Containing the best Jokes
and Gems of Wit, composed and delivered by the favorite Equestrian Clown,
Ned Turner. Selected and arranged by G. E. G...................10 cts.

Charley White's Joke Book. Containing a full exposé of all
the most laughable Jokes, Witticisms, etc., as told by the celebrated
Ethiopian Comedian, Charles White...............................10 cts.

Black Wit and Darky Conversations. By Charles White.
Containing a large collection of laughable Anecdotes, Jokes, Stories, Witticisms and Darky Conversations.....................................10 cts.

Yale College Scrapes; or, How the Boys Go It at New
Haven. This is a book of 114 pages, containing accounts of all the famous
"Scrapes" and "Sprees" of which students of Old Yale have been
guilty for the last quarter of a century ....25 cts.

Laughing Gas. An Encyclopedia of Wit, Wisdom and Wind.
By Sam Slick, Jr. Comically illustrated with 100 original and laughable
Engravings, and nearly 500 side-extending Jokes.................30 cts.

The Knapsack Full of Fun; or, 1,000 Rations of Laughter.
Illustrated with over 100 comical engravings, and containing Jokes and
Funny Stories. By Doesticks and other witty writers. Large quarto..30 cts.

The Comical Adventures of David Dufficks. Illustrated with
over one hundred Funny Engravings. This is a book full of fun....25 cts.

The Plate of Chowder. A Dish for Funny Fellows. Appro-
priately illustrated with 100 comic engravings. 12mo, paper covers..25 cts.

The Young Debater and Chairman's Assistant. By an ex-
Member of the Philadelphia Bar. Containing instructions how to Form and Conduct Societies; how to Form and Conduct Clubs and other organized Associations; Rules of Order for the Government of their Business and Debates; how to Compose Resolutions, Reports and Petitions; how to Organize and Manage Public Meetings, Celebrations, Dinners, Pic-Nics and Conventions; Duties of the President and other Officers of a Club or Society, with Official Forms; Hints on Debate and Public Speaking; Forms for Constitutions and By-Laws. To any one who desires to become familiar with the duties of an Officer or Committee-man in a Society or Association this work will be invaluable, as it contains the most minute instructions in everything that pertains to the routine of Society Business.
152 pages, paper covers...30 cts.
Bound in boards, with cloth back.......... ....50 cts.

How to Conduct a Debate. A Series of Complete Debates,
Outlines of Debates and Questions for Discussion. In the complete debates, the questions for discussion are defined, the debate formally opened, an array of brilliant arguments adduced on either side, and the debate closed according to parliamentary usages. The second part consists of questions for debate, with heads of arguments, for and against, given in a condensed form, for the speakers to enlarge upon to suit their own fancy. In addition to these are a large collection of debatable questions. The authorities to be referred to for information being given at the close of every debate throughout the work. By Frederic Rowton. 232 pages, 16mo.
Paper covers...50 cts.
Bound in boards, cloth back.......................................75 cts.

The Vegetable Garden. Containing thorough instructions for
Sowing, Planting and Cultivating all kinds of Vegetables, with plain directions for preparing, manuring and tilling the soil to suit each plant; including, also, a summary of the work to be done in a Vegetable Garden during each month of the year. This work embraces, in a condensed but thoroughly practical form, all the information that either an amateur or a practical gardener can require in connection with the successful raising of Vegetables and Herbs. It also gives separate directions for the cultivation of some seventy different Vegetables, including all the varieties of esculents that form the ordinary stock of a kitchen garden or truck farm. By James Hogg.
140 pages, paper covers.................... ....30 cts.
Full cloth................... ....50 cts.

The Amateur Trapper and Trap-Maker's Guide. A com-
plete and carefully prepared treatise on the art of Trapping, Snaring and Netting. This comprehensive work is embellished with fifty engraved illustrations; and these, together with the clear explanations which accompany them, will enable anybody of moderate comprehension to make and set any of the traps described. It also gives the baits usually employed by the most successful Hunters and Trappers, and exposes their secret methods of attracting and catching animals, birds, etc., with scarcely a possibility of failure. Large 16mo, paper covers.... ....50 cts.
Bound in boards, cloth back.......................................75 cts.

How to Write a Composition. The use of this excellent hand-
book will save the student the many hours of labor too often wasted in trying to write a plain composition. It affords a perfect skeleton of one hundred and seventeen different subjects, with their headings or divisions clearly defined, and each heading filled in with the ideas which the subject suggests; so that all the writer has to do, in order to produce a good composition, is to enlarge on them to suit his taste and inclination.
178 pages, paper covers..30 cts.
Bound in boards, cloth back.......................................50 cts.

Barber's American Book of Ready-Made Speeches.

Containing 159 original examples of Humorous and Serious Speeches, suitable for every possible occasion where a speech may be called for, together with appropriate replies to each. Including:

Presentation Speeches.	*Off-Hand Speeches on a Variety of*
Convivial Speeches.	*Subjects.*
Festival Speeches.	*Miscellaneous Speeches.*
Addresses of Congratulation.	*Toasts and Sentiments for Public and*
Addresses of Welcome.	*Private Entertainments.*
Addresses of Compliment.	*Preambles and Resolutions of Con-*
Political Speeches.	*gratulation, Compliment and Con-*
Dinner and Supper Speeches for Clubs,	*dolence.*
etc.	

With this book any person may prepare himself to make a neat little speech, or reply to one when called upon to do so. They are all short, appropriate and witty, and even ready speakers may profit by them. Paper....50 cts.
Bound in boards, cloth back.................................. ....75 cts.

Day's American Ready-Reckoner.

By B. H. Day. This Ready-Reckoner is composed of Original Tables, which are positively correct, having been revised in the most careful manner. It is a book of 192 pages, and embraces more matter than 500 pages of any other Reckoner. It contains: Tables for Rapid Calculations of Aggregate Values, Wages, Salaries, Board, Interest Money, etc.; Tables of Timber and Plank Measurement; Tables of Board and Log Measurement, and a great variety of Tables and useful calculations which it would be impossible to enumerate in an advertisement of this limited space. All the information in this valuable book is given in a simple manner, and is made so plain, that any person can use it at once without any previous study or loss of time.
Bound in boards, with cloth back....... ....50 cts.
Bound in cloth, gilt back................. ....75 cts.

The Art and Etiquette of Making Love.

A Manual of Love, Courtship and Matrimony. It tells

How to cure bashfulness,	*How to break off an engagement,*
How to commence a courtship,	*How to act after an engagement,*
How to please a sweetheart or lover,	*How to act as bridesmaid or grooms-*
How to write a love-letter,	*man,*
How to "pop the question,"	*How the etiquette of a wedding and the*
How to act before and after a proposal,	*after reception should be observed,*
How to accept or reject a proposal,	

And, in fact, how to fulfill every duty and meet every contingency connected with courtship and matrimony. 176 pages. Paper covers ....30 cts.
Bound in boards, cloth back.................................50 cts.

Frank Converse's Complete Banjo Instructor Without a Master.

Containing a choice collection of Banjo Solos and Hornpipes, Walk Arounds, Reels and Jigs, Songs and Banjo Stories, progressively arranged and plainly explained, enabling the learner to become a proficient banjoist without the aid of a teacher. The necessary explanations accompany each tune, and are placed under the notes on each page, plainly showing the string required, the finger to be used for stopping it, the manner of striking, and the number of times it must be sounded. The Instructor is illustrated with diagrams and explanatory symbols. 100 pages. Bound in boards, cloth back...................................... ....50 cts.

Hard Words Made Easy.

Rules for Pronunciation and Accent; with instructions how to pronounce French, Italian, German, Spanish, and other foreign names........ ....12 cts.

Rarey & Knowlson's Complete Horse Tamer and Farrier.

A New and Improved Edition, containing: Mr. Rarey's Whole Secret of Subduing and Breaking Vicious Horses; His Improved Plan of Managing Young Colts, and Breaking them to the Saddle, to Harness and the Sulky. Rules for Selecting a Good Horse, and for Feeding Horses. Also the Complete Farrier or Horse Doctor; being the result of fifty years' extensive practice of the author, John C. Knowlson, during his life an English Farrier of high popularity; containing the latest discoveries in the cure of Spavin. Illustrated with descriptive engravings. Bound in boards, cloth back..50 cts.

How to Amuse an Evening Party. A Complete collection of

Home Recreations. Profusely Illustrated with over Two Hundred fine wood-cuts, containing Round Games and Forfeit Games, Parlor Magic and Curious Puzzles, Comic Diversions and Parlor Tricks, Scientific Recreations and Evening Amusements. A young man with this volume may render himself the *beau ideal* of a delightful companion at every party, and win the hearts of all the ladies, by his powers of entertainment. Bound in ornamental paper covers..30 cts.
Bound in boards, with cloth back...............................50 cts.

Frost's Laws and By-Laws of American Society. A Com-

plete Treatise on Etiquette. Containing plain and Reliable Directions for Deportment in every Situation in Life, by S. A. Frost, author of "Frost's Letter-Writer," etc. This is a book of ready reference on the usages of Society at all times and on all occasions, and also a reliable guide in the details of deportment and polite behavior. Paper covers.................30 cts.
Bound in boards, with cloth back...............................50 cts.

Frost's Original Letter-Writer. A complete collection of Orig-

inal Letters and Notes, upon every imaginable subject of Every-Day Life, with plain directions about everything connected with writing a letter. By S. A. Frost. To which is added a comprehensive Table of Synonyms, alone worth double the price asked for the book. We assure our readers that it is the best collection of letters ever published in this country; they are written in plain and natural language, and elegant in style without being high-flown. Bound in boards, cloth back, with illuminated sides.................50 cts.

North's Book of Love-Letters. With directions how to write

and when to use them, and 120 Specimen Letters, suitable for Lovers of any age and condition, and under all circumstances. Interspersed with the author's comments thereon. The whole forming a convenient Hand-book of valuable information and counsel for the use of those who need friendly guidance and advice in matters of Love, Courtship and Marriage. By Ingoldsby North. Bound in boards..50 cts.
Bound in cloth...75 cts.

How to Shine in Society; or, The Science of Conversation.

Containing the principles, laws and general usages of polite society, including easily applied hints and directions for commencing and sustaining an agreeable conversation, and for choosing topics appropriate to the time, place and company, thus affording immense assistance to the bashful and diffident. 16mo. Paper covers..25 cts.

The Poet's Companion. A Dictionary of all Allowable Rhymes

in the English Language. This gives the Perfect, the Imperfect and Allowable Rhymes, and will enable you to ascertain to a certainty whether any word can be mated. It is invaluable to any one who desires to court the Muses, and is used by some of the best writers in the country.......25 cts.

Mind Your Stops. Punctuation made plain, and Composition

simplified for Readers, Writers and Talkers.......................12 cts.

Five Hundred French Phrases. A book giving all the French

words and maxims in general use in writing the English language...12 cts.

Sut Lovingood. Yarns spun by "A Nat'ral Born Durn'd Fool."

Warped and Wove for Public Wear, by George W. Harris. Illustrated with eight fine full page engravings, from designs by Howard. It would be difficult, we think, to cram a larger amount of pungent humor into 300 pages than will be found in this really funny book. The Preface and Dedication are models of sly simplicity, and the 24 Sketches which follow are among the best specimens of broad burlesque to which the genius of the ludicrous, for which the Southwest is so distinguished, has yet given birth. 12mo, tinted paper, cloth, gilt edges.................................$1.50

Uncle Josh's Trunkful of Fun. Containing a rich collection of

Comical Stories, Cruel Sells, Side-Splitting Jokes, Humorous Poetry, Quaint Parodies, Burlesque Sermons,	New Conundrums, Mirth-Provoking Speeches, Curious Puzzles, Amusing Card Tricks, and Astonishing Feats of Parlor-Magic.

This book is illustrated with nearly 200 funny engravings, and contains, in 64 large octavo double-column pages, at least three times as much reading matter and real fun as any other book of the price.................. 15 cts.

The Strange and Wonderful Adventures of Bachelor

Butterfly. Showing how his passion for Natural History completely eradicated the tender passion implanted in his breast—also detailing his Extraordinary Travels, both by sea and land—his Hair-breadth Escapes from fire and cold—his being come over by a Widow with nine small children—his wonderful Adventures with the Doctor and the Fiddler, and other Perils of a most extraordinary nature. The whole illustrated by about 200 engravings.................................30 cts,

The Laughable Adventures of Messrs. Brown, Jones and

Robinson. Showing where they went, and how they went, what they did, and how they did it. Here is a book which will make you split your sides laughing. It shows the comical adventures of three jolly young greenhorns, who went traveling, and got into all manner of scrapes and funny adventures. Illustrated with nearly 200 thrillingly-comic engravings.....30 cts.

The Mishaps and Adventures of Obadiah Oldbuck. This

humorous and curious book sets forth, with 188 comic drawings, the misfortunes which befell Mr. Oldbuck; and also his five unsuccessful attempts to commit suicide—his hair-breadth escapes from fire, water and famine—his affection for his poor dog, etc. To look over this book will make you laugh, and you can't help it..30 cts.

Jack Johnson's Jokes for the Jolly. A collection of Funny

Stories, Droll Incidents, Queer Conceits and Apt Repartees. Illustrating the Drolleries of Border Life in the West, Yankee Peculiarities, Dutch Blunders, French Sarcasms, Irish Wit and Humor. etc., with short Ludicrous Narratives; making altogether a Medley of Mirthful Morsels for the Melancholy that will drive away the blues, and cause the most misanthropic mortal to laugh. Illustrated paper covers.......................25 cts.

Snipsnaps and Snickerings of Simon Snodgrass. A collec-

tion of Droll and Laughable Stories, illustrative of Irish Drolleries and Blarney, Ludicrous Dutch Blunders, Queer Yankee Tricks and Dodges, Backwoods Boasting, Humors of Horse-trading, Negro Comicalities, Perilous Pranks of Fighting Men, Frenchmen's Queer Mistakes, Scotch Shrewdness, and other phases of eccentric character, that go to make up a perfect and complete Medley of Wit and Humor. It is also full of funny engravings.......................................25 cts.

Madame Le Normand's Fortune Teller. An entertaining
book, said to have been written by Madame Le Normand, the celebrated
French Fortune Teller, who was frequently consulted by the Emperor
Napoleon. A party of ladies and gentlemen may amuse themselves for
hours with this curious book. It tells fortunes by "The Chart of Fate" (a
large lithographic chart), and gives 624 answers to questions on every imaginable subject that may happen in the future. It explains a variety of ways
for telling fortunes by Cards and Dice; gives a list of 79 curious old su-
perstitions and omens, and 187 weather omens, and winds up with the celebrated Oraculum of Napoleon. We will not endorse this book as infallible;
but we assure our readers that it is the source of much mirth whenever introduced at a gathering of ladies and gentlemen. Bound in boards.40 cts.

The Fireside Magician; or, The Art of Natural Magic
Made Easy. Being a scientific explanation of Legerdemain, Physical
Amusement, Recreative Chemistry, Diversion with Cards, and of all the
mysteries of Mechanical Magic, with feats as performed by Herr Alexander,
Robert Heller, Robert Houdin, "The Wizard of the North," and distin-
guished conjurors—comprising two hundred and fifty interesting mental and
physical recreations, with explanatory engravings. 132 pages, paper.30 cts.
Bound in boards, cloth back..50 cts.

Howard's Book of Conundrums and Riddles. Containing
over 1,200 of the best Conundrums, Riddles, Enigmas, Ingenious Catches
and Amusing Sells ever invented. This splendid collection of curious paradoxes will afford the material for a never-ending feast of fun and amusement.
Any person, with the assistance of this book, may take the lead in entertaining a company, and keep them in roars of laughter for hours together.
Paper covers...... ....30 cts.
Bound in boards, cloth back..50 cts.

The Parlor Magician; or, One Hundred Tricks for the
Drawing-Room. Containing an extensive and miscellaneous collection of
Conjuring and Legerdemain, embracing: Tricks with Dice, Dominoes and
Cards; Tricks with Ribbons, Rings and Fruit; Tricks with Coin, Hand-
kerchiefs and Balls, etc. The whole illustrated and clearly explained with
121 engravings. Paper covers...30 cts.
Bound in boards, with cloth back.......................................50 cts.

Book of Riddles and 500 Home Amusements. Containing
a curious collection of Riddles, Charades and Enigmas; Rebuses, Anagrams
and Transpositions; Conundrums and Amusing Puzzles; Recreations in
Arithmetic, and Queer Sleights, and numerous other Entertaining Amusements. Illustrated with 60 engravings. Paper covers..............30 cts.
Bound in boards, with cloth back....... ....50 cts.

The Book of Fireside Games. Containing an explanation of a
variety of Witty, Rollicking, Entertaining and Innocent Games and Amusing Forfeits, suited to the Family Circle as a Recreation. This book is just
the thing for social gatherings, parties and pic-nics. Paper covers .30 cts.
Bound in boards, cloth back..50 cts.

The Book of 500 Curious Puzzles. Containing a large collec-
tion of Curious Puzzles, Entertaining Paradoxes, Perplexing Deceptions in
Numbers, Amusing Tricks in Geometry; illustrated with a great variety of
Engravings. Paper covers...30 cts.
Bound in boards, with cloth back......................................50 cts.

Parlor Tricks with Cards. Containing explanations of all the
Tricks and Deceptions with Playing Cards ever invented. The whole illus-
trated and made plain and easy with 70 engravings. Paper covers..30 cts.
Bound in boards, with cloth back......................................50 cts.

Day's Book-Keeping Without a Master. Containing the Rudiments of Book-keeping in Single and Double Entry, together with the proper Forms and Rules for opening and keeping condensed and general Book Accounts. This work is printed in a beautiful script type, and hence combines the advantages of a handsome style of writing with its very simple and easily understood lessons in Book-keeping. The several pages have explanations at the bottom to assist the learner, in small type. As a pattern for opening book accounts it is especially valuable—particularly for those who are not well posted in the art. DAY'S BOOK-KEEPING is the size of a regular quarto Account Book, and is made to lie flat open for convenience in use ....50 cts.

Blank Books for Day's Book-Keeping. We have for sale Books of 96 pages each, ruled according to the patterns mentioned on page 3 of DAY'S BOOK-KEEPING, suitable for practice of the learner, viz.: No. 1— For General Book-keeping, pages 4 and 5; for Cash Account on page 13; for Day-Book in Single Entry, pages 15 to 25. No. 2—For Condensed Accounts, pages 9 and 10; for Cash Account, page 12; for Journal in Double Entry, pages 34 to 43. No. 3—For Ledgers in Double or Single Entry, pages 26 to 44. Each Number ....50 cts.

How to Learn the Sense of 3,000 French Words in one Hour. This ingenious little book actually accomplishes all that its title claims. It is a fact that there are at least three thousand words in the French language, forming a large proportion of those used in ordinary conversation, which are spelled exactly the same as in English, or become the same by very slight and easily understood changes in their termination. 16-mo, illuminated paper covers ....25 cts.

How to Speak in Public; or, The Art of Extempore Oratory. A valuable manual for those who desire to become ready off-hand speakers; containing clear directions how to arrange ideas logically and quickly, including illustrations, by the analysis of speeches delivered by some of the greatest orators, exemplifying the importance of correct emphasis, clearness of articulation, and appropriate gesture. Paper covers ....25 cts.

Live and Learn. A guide for all those who wish to speak and write correctly; particularly intended as a Book of Reference for the solution of difficulties connected with Grammar, Composition, Punctuation, &c., &c., containing examples of 1,000 mistakes of daily occurrence in speaking, writing and pronunciation. Cloth, 16mo, 216 pages............75 cts.

The Art of Dressing Well. By Miss S. A. Frost. This book is designed for ladies and gentlemen who desire to make a favorable impression upon society. Paper covers....................................30 cts. Bound in boards, cloth back...................................50 cts.

Thimm's French Self-Taught. A new system, on the most simple principles, for Universal Self-Tuition, with English pronunciation of every word. By this system the acquirement of the French Language is rendered less laborious and more thorough than by any of the old methods. By Franz Thimm ....25 cts.

Thimm's German Self-Taught. Uniform with "French Self-Taught," and arranged in accordance with the same principles of thoroughness and simplicity. By Franz Thimm..............................25 cts.

Thimm's Spanish Self-Taught. A book of self-instruction in the Spanish Language, arranged according to the same method as the "French" and "German," by the same author, and uniform with them in size. By Franz Thimm..25 cts.

Thimm's Italian Self-Taught. Uniform in style and size with the three foregoing books. By Franz Thimm....................25 cts.

Martine's Sensible Letter-Writer.

Being a comprehensive and complete Guide and Assistant for those who desire to carry on Epistolary Correspondence; containing a large collection of model letters on the simplest matters of life, adapted to all ages and conditions—

EMBRACING,

Business Letters; Applications for Employment, with Letters of Recommendation and Answers to Advertisements; Letters between Parents and Children; Letters of Friendly Counsel and Remonstrance; Letters soliciting Advice, Assistance and Friendly Favors;

Letters of Courtesy, Friendship and Affection; Letters of Condolence and Sympathy; A Choice Collection of Love-Letters, for Every Situation in a Courtship; Notes of Ceremony, Familiar Invitations, etc., together with Notes of Acceptance and Regret.

The whole containing 300 Sensible Letters and Notes. This is an invaluable book for those persons who have not had sufficient practice to enable them to write letters without great effort. It contains such a variety of letters, that models may be found to suit every subject.

297 pages, bound in boards, cloth back.............................50 cts.
Bound in cloth...75 cts.

Martine's Hand-Book of Etiquette and Guide to True Politeness.

A complete Manual for all those who desire to understand good breeding, the customs of good society, and to avoid incorrect and vulgar habits. Containing clear and comprehensive directions for correct manners, conversation, dress, introductions, rules for good behavior at Dinner Parties and the Table, with hints on carving and wine at table; together with the Etiquette of the Ball and Assembly Room, Evening Parties, and the usages to be observed when visiting or receiving calls; Deportment in the street and when traveling. To which is added the Etiquette of Courtship, Marriage, Domestic Duties and fifty-six rules to be observed in general society. By Arthur Martine. Bound in boards ..50 cts.
Bound in cloth, gilt sides.................................75 cts.

Dick's Quadrille Call-Book and Ball-Room Prompter.

Containing clear directions how to call out the figures of every dance, with the quantity of music necessary for each figure, and simple explanations of all the figures which occur in Plain and Fancy Quadrilles. This book gives plain and comprehensive instructions how to dance all the new and popular dances, including the following:

The Parisian Varieties;
The New French Quadrille;
The Waltz Quadrille;
The Glide Lancers;
The Saratoga Lancers;
The Waltz Caledonians;
The Prince Imperial;
The Caledonians and Lancers;
The Social, Basket and Gavotte Quadrilles;

The Empire Quadrille;
The March, Star and Mazurka Quadrilles;
The Cheat and Jig, London Polka, and other Plain and Fancy Quadrilles;
All the Round Dances, Reels and Country Dances;
The "German," with description of the new Figures.

To which is added a Complete and Sensible Guide for Etiquette and Proper Deportment in the Ball and Assembly Room, besides 108 pages of dance music for the piano. Paper covers.............................50 cts.
Bound in boards.................................75 cts.

Wright's Book of 3,000 American Receipts.

Containing Cookery, Distilling, Perfumery, Chemicals, Varnishes, Dyeing, Agriculture, etc. 12mo, cloth, 350 pages.............................$1.50

Lola Montez' Arts of Beauty; or, Secrets of a Lady's

Toilet. *With hints to Gentlemen on the Art of Fascinating.* Lola Montez here explains all the Arts employed by the celebrated beauties and fashionable ladies in Paris and other cities of Europe, for the purpose of preserving their beauty and improving and developing their charms. The recipes are all clearly given, so that any person can understand them, and the work embraces the following subjects: .

How to obtain such desirable and indispensable attractions as A Handsome Form ;	*A Soft and Abundant Head of Hair; Also, How to Remedy Gray Hair; And harmless but effectual methods of*
A Bright and Smooth Skin ;	*removing Superfluous Hair and*
A Beautiful Complexion ;	*other blemishes, with interesting in-*
Attractive Eyes, Mouth and Lips ;	*formation on these and kindred*
A Beautiful Hand, Foot and Ankle ;	*matters.*
A Well-trained Voice ;	

Illuminated paper cover...25 cts.

Hillgrove's Ball-Room Guide and Complete Dancing-

Master. Containing a plain treatise on Etiquette and Deportment at Balls and Parties, with valuable hints on Dress and the Toilet, together with

Full Explanations of the Rudiments, Terms, Figures and Steps used in Dancing;	*Reels, Round, Plain and Fancy Dances, so that any person may learn them without the aid of a*
Including Clear and Precise Instructions how to dance all kinds of Quadrilles, Waltzes, Polkas, Redowas,	*Teacher; To which is added easy directions how to call out the Figures*

of every dance, and the amount of music required for each. Illustrated with 176 descriptive engravings. By T. Hillgrove, Professor of Dancing. Bound in cloth, with gilt side and back..............................$1.00
Bound in boards, with cloth back...............................75 cts.

The Banjo, and How to Play it.

Containing, in addition to the elementary studies, a choice collection of Polkas, Waltzes, Solos, Schottisches, Songs, Hornpipes, Jigs, Reels, etc., with full explanations of both the "Banjo" and "Guitar" styles of execution, and designed to impart a complete knowledge of the art of playing the Banjo practically, without the aid of a teacher. This work is arranged on the progressive system, showing the learner how to play the first few notes of a tune, then the next notes, and so on, a small portion at a time, until he has mastered the entire piece, every detail being as clearly and thoroughly explained as if he had a teacher at his elbow all the time. By Frank B. Converse, author of the "Banjo without a Master." 16mo, bound in boards, cloth back..50 cts.

Row's National Wages Tables.

Showing at a glance the amount of wages from half an hour to sixty hours, at from $1 to $37 per week. Also from one-quarter of a day to four weeks, at $1 to $37 per week. By Nelson Row. By this book, which is particularly useful when part of a week, day or hour is lost, a large pay-roll can be made out in a few minutes, thus saving more time in making out one pay-roll than the cost of the book. Every employer hiring help by the hour, day or week, and every employee, should obtain one, as it will enable him to know exactly the amount of money he is entitled to on pay-day. Half bound....................50 cts.

Row's Complete Fractional Ready-Reckoner.

For buying and selling any kind of merchandise, giving the fractional parts of a pound, yard, etc., from one-quarter to one thousand, at any price from one-quarter of a cent to five dollars. By Nelson Row. 36mo, 232 pages, boards..50 cts.

Blunders in Behavior Corrected.

A book of Deportment for both Ladies and Gentlemen. By means of this book you can learn the most difficult phases in Etiquette, or behavior in good society............13 cts.

Delisser's Horseman's Guide.

Comprising the Laws on Warranty, and the Rules in purchasing and selling horses, with the decisions and reports of various courts in Europe and the United States; to which is added a detailed account of what constitutes soundness and unsoundness, and a precise method, simply laid down, for the examination of horses, showing their age to thirty years old; together with an exposure of the various tricks and impositions practiced by low horse-dealers (jockeys) on inexperienced persons; also, a valuable Table of each and every bone in the structure of the Horse. By George P. Delisser, Veterinary Surgeon.
Bound in boards, cloth back.....................................75 cts.
Bound in cloth...$1.00

Brisbane's Golden Ready-Reckoner.

Calculated in Dollars and Cents. Showing at once the amount or value of any number of articles or quantity of goods, or any merchandise, either by the gallon, quart, pint, ounce, pound, quarter, hundred, yard, foot, inch, bushel, etc., in an easy and plain manner. To which are added Interest Tables, calculated in dollars and cents, for days and for months, at six per cent. and at seven per cent. per annum, alternately; and a great number of other Tables and Rules for calculation never before in print. Bound in boards.................35 cts.

How to Cook Potatoes, Apples, Eggs and Fish, Four

Hundred Different Ways. Our lady friends will be surprised when they examine this book, and find the great variety of ways that the same article may be prepared and cooked. The work especially recommends itself to those who are often embarrassed for want of variety in dishes suitable for the breakfast-table, or on occasions where the necessity arises for preparing a meal at short notice. Paper covers.............................30 cts.
Bound in boards, with cloth back..............................50 cts.

The American Housewife and Kitchen Directory.

This valuable book embraces three hundred and seventy-eight recipes for cooking all sorts of American dishes in the most economical manner; it also contains a variety of important secrets for washing, cleaning, scouring and extracting grease, paint, stains and iron-mould from cloth, muslin and linen. Bound in ornamental paper covers...30 cts.
Bound in boards, with cloth back..............................50 cts.

How to Cook and How to Carve.

Giving plain and easily understood directions for preparing and cooking, with the greatest economy, every kind of dish, with complete instructions for serving the same. This book is just the thing for a young Housekeeper. It is worth a dozen of expensive French books. Paper covers..............................30 cts.
Bound in boards, with cloth back..............................50 cts.

The American Home Cook Book.

Containing several hundred excellent recipes. The whole based on many years' experience of an American Housewife. Illustrated with engravings. All the Recipes in this book are written from actual experience in Cooking. Paper....30 cts.
Bound in boards, cloth back................................50 cts.

The Yankee Cook Book.

A new system of Cookery. Containing hundreds of excellent recipes from actual experience in Cooking; also, full explanations in the art of Carving. 126 pages, paper covers.30 cts.
Bound in boards, with cloth back..............................50 cts.

How to Mix all Kinds of Fancy Drinks.

Containing clear and reliable directions for mixing all the beverages used in the United States. Embracing Punches, Juleps, Cobblers, Cocktails, etc., etc., in endless variety. By Jerry Thomas. Illuminated paper covers......................50 cts.
Bound in full cloth...75 cts.

What Shall We Do To-Night? or, Social Amusements for
Evening Parties. This elegant book affords an almost inexhaustible fund of amusement for evening parties, social gatherings and all festive occasions, ingeniously grouped together so as to furnish complete and ever-varying entertainment for Twenty-six evenings. Its repertoire embraces all the best round and forfeit games, clearly described and rendered perfectly plain by original and amusing examples, interspersed with a great variety of ingenious puzzles, entertaining tricks and innocent sells; new and original Musical and Poetical pastimes, startling illusions and mirth-provoking exhibitions; including complete directions and text for performing Charades, Tableaux, Parlor Pantomimes, the world-renowned Punch and Judy, Gallanty Shows and original Shadow-pantomimes; also, full information for the successful performance of Dramatic Dialogues and Parlor Theatricals, with a selection of Original Plays, etc., written expressly for this work. It is embellished with over one hundred descriptive and explanatory engravings, and contains 366 pages, printed on fine toned paper. Extra cloth...$2.00

The Secret Out: or, 1,000 Tricks with Cards, and Other
Recreations. Illustrated with over 300 engravings. A book which explains all the Tricks and Deceptions with Playing Cards ever known, and gives, besides, a great many new ones. The whole being described so carefully, with engravings to illustrate them, that anybody can easily learn how to perform them. This work also contains 240 of the best Tricks of Legerdemain, in addition to the Card Tricks. Such is the unerring process of instruction adopted in this volume, that no reader can fail to succeed in executing every Trick, Experiment, Game, etc., set down, if he will at all devote his attention, in his leisure hours, to the subject; and, as almost every trick with cards known will be found in this collection, it may be considered the only complete work on the subject ever published 12mo, 400 pages, bound in cloth, gilt side and back.................$1.50

The Magician's Own Book; or, The Whole Art of Conjuring. A complete hand-book of Parlor Magic, containing over a thousand Optical, Chemical, Mechanical, Magnetic and Magical Experiments, Amusing Transmutations, Astonishing Sleights and Subtleties, Celebrated Card Deceptions, Ingenious Tricks with Numbers, curious and entertaining Puzzles, the Art of Secret Writing, together with all the most noted tricks of modern performers. Illustrated with over 500 wood-cuts, the whole forming a comprehensive guide for amateurs. 12mo, cloth, gilt... ..$1.50

The Sociable; or, One Thousand and One Home Amusements. Containing Acting Proverbs, Dramatic Charades, Acting Charades or Drawing-room Pantomimes, Musical Burlesques, Tableaux Vivants, Parlor Games, Games of Action, Forfeits, Science in Sport and Parlor Magic, and a choice collection of curious Mental and Mechanical Puzzles, etc. Illustrated with numerous engravings and diagrams. The whole being a fund of never-ending entertainment. 376 pages, cloth, gilt......$1.50

Athletic Sports for Boys. A Repository of Graceful Recreations for Youth, containing clear and complete instructions in Gymnastics, Limb Exercises, Jumping, Pole-Leaping, Dumb Bells, Indian Clubs, Parallel Bars, the Horizontal Bar, the Trapeze, the Suspended Ropes, and the manly accomplishments of Skating, Swimming, Rowing, Sailing, Horsemanship, Riding, Driving, Angling, Fencing and Broadsword. Illustrated with 194 wood-cuts. Bound in boards............................75 cts.

The Young Reporter; or, How to Write Short-Hand. A
Complete Phonographic Teacher, intended as a School-book, to afford thorough instructions to those who have not the assistance of an Oral Teacher. By the aid of this work, any person of the most ordinary intelligence may learn to write Short-Hand, and report Speeches and Sermons in a short time. Bound in boards, with cloth back............ ....50 cts.

www.ingramcontent.com/pod-product-compliance
Lightning Source LLC
Chambersburg PA
CBHW022359020726
47500CB00002B/354